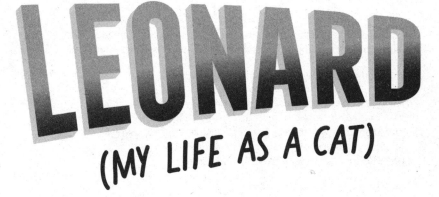

LEONARD
(MY LIFE AS A CAT)

CARLIE SOROSIAK

WALKER BOOKS

First US paperback edition 2022
First published by Nosy Crow (UK) 2020

Library of Congress Catalog Card Number 2021933904
ISBN 978-1-5362-0770-5 (hardcover)
ISBN 978-1-5362-2581-5 (paperback)

TRC 27 26 25 24 23 22
10 9 8 7 6 5 4 3 2 1

Printed in Eagan, MN, USA

This book was typeset in Droid Serif.

Walker Books US
a division of
Candlewick Press
99 Dover Street
Somerville, Massachusetts 02144

www.walkerbooksus.com

*To Mom,
who filled our home with love—
and with cats*

Look again at that dot. That's here. That's home. That's us.

—Carl Sagan

Humans have it all wrong about aliens. Sometimes
I see images of us on television—with enormous eyes,
with skin the color of spring leaves—and I wonder:
Who thought of this? What reason could they have?
Olive always tells me not to watch those shows. "You'll
just give yourself bad dreams," she says. So we switch
off the TV and curl up by the window, listening to the
gentle hush of waves.

But the truth is, I really don't belong here—not
permanently, not forever. That's why we're traveling in this Winnebago, zooming down dark roads at
midnight. Olive is wearing her frayed overalls, and
she's cradling me in her arms.

I don't squirm. I don't scratch. I am not that type
of cat.

"You won't forget me," she says, pressing her forehead to mine. "Please promise you won't."

She smells of cinnamon toast and raspberry shampoo. There are daisy barrettes in her hair. And for a second, I consider lying to her—out of love. The words are right there: *I will always remember. I could never forget.* But I've been honest with her this whole time, and the rules of intergalactic travel are clear.

Tomorrow, I will forget everything I've ever felt.

In my mind, Olive will exist only as data, as pure information. I'll remember her daisy barrettes, our Saturday afternoons by Wrigley Pier—but not how it felt to share a beach towel, or read books together, or fall asleep under the late June sun. And Olive doesn't deserve that. She is so much more than a collection of facts.

Halfheartedly, I summon a purr. It rattles weakly in my chest.

"You get to go home," Olive says, the ghost of a smile on her face. "Home."

The Winnebago speeds faster, then faster still. Outside, the sky is full of stars. And I want to communicate that I will miss this—feeling so small, so *earthly*. Am I ready to go back? Half of me is. And yet, when I close my eyes, I picture myself clinging to the walls of this motor home.

Olive sets me down on the countertop, the plastic cool under my paws. Opening her laptop, she angles the keyboard toward me, a gesture that says, *Type, will you?* But I shake my head, fur shivering.

"You don't want to talk?" she asks.

What can I say? I owe it to Olive not to make this any harder. So I won't use the computer. I won't tell her what I've been hoping—to maybe carry one thing back. Maybe if I concentrate hard enough, a part of Olive will imprint on a part of me, and I will remember how it felt. How it felt to know a girl once.

"Okay," she says, shutting her laptop with a sigh. "At least eat your crunchies."

So I eat my crunchies. They're trout-flavored and tangy on my tongue. I chew slowly, savoring the morsels. This is one of my last meals as a cat.

I haven't always lived in this body. Leonard wasn't always my name.

Olive pats my head as I lick the bowl clean. "I know you didn't want to be a cat," she says, so softly that my ears prick to hear her, "but you are a very, very good cat."

I want the computer now. My paws are itching to

type: *You are a very, very good human.* Because she is. And she will be, long after I'm gone.

If you allow yourself, you might like our story. It's about cheese sandwiches and an aquarium and a family. It has laughter and sadness and me, learning what it means to be human.

On my journey to Earth, I was supposed to become human.

That is where I'll begin.

For almost three hundred years, I had wished for hands. Every once in a while, I pictured myself holding an object in my own palm, with my own fingers. An apple, a book, an umbrella. I'd heard the most wonderful rumors about umbrellas—and *rain*, how it dotted your skin. Humans might take these things for granted (standing in the street, half shielded by an umbrella in a summer rainstorm), but I promised myself, centuries ago, that I would not.

It was all just so tremendously exciting, as I hitched a ride on that beam of light.

This trip to Earth was about discovery, about glimpsing another way of life.

And I was ready.

On the eve of our three hundredth birthdays, all members of our species have the opportunity to spend a month as an Earth creature—to expand our minds, gather data, and keep an eye on the neighbors. I could've been a penguin in Antarctica or a wild beast roaming the plains of the Serengeti; I could've been a beluga whale or a wolf or a goose. Instead, I chose the most magnificent creature on Earth: the common human.

Perhaps you find my decision laughable. I feel the need to defend it. So please think about penguins, who refuse to play the violin. About wolves, who have no use for umbrellas. Even geese take little joy in the arts. But humans? Humans write books, and share thoughts over coffee, and make things for absolutely zero reason. Swimming pools, doorbells, elevators—I was dying to discover the delight of them all.

Still, it was a terrifically difficult choice, narrowing it down. Because there are so many different *types* of humans. Did I want to wear shorts and deliver mail? Would a hairnet look flattering on me? Could I convincingly become a television star? After nearly fifty years of thought, I decided on something humbler. More suited to my interests.

A national park ranger. A *Yellowstone* ranger. Wasn't it perfect? I'd give myself a mustache and boots and have a dazzling twinkle in my left eye. In my mind, I'd practiced the way I'd flick my wrists—I'd have wrists, you see—toward the natural exhibits. In front of a crowd of human tourists, I'd walk with an exaggerated swing of my hips and carry many useful things in my pockets: a Swiss Army knife, a butterfly net, a variety of pens for writing. Humor is a valued trait among humans, so for an entire year, I exclusively prepared jokes.

How many park rangers does it take to change a light bulb? Twenty-two. Do you get it? *Twenty-two!* (I wasn't entirely sure that I understood humor; my species is pure energy and can't exactly feel in our natural state. But wasn't there something inherently funny about the curve of a two, let alone two twos?)

Setting off from my home planet, I imagined the feeling of laughter, how it might rattle my belly. It was a nice distraction, considering the strangeness of it all. My species is a hive mind, meaning we think and exist as one, like drops in the ocean of Earth—and I wasn't prepared for the sensation of leaving them. There was a quiet *pop* as we separated. Then I was alone, for the first time in three hundred years.

Honestly, I wasn't entirely sure what to do with myself. In the distance were the crystallized mountains of my planet, rivers of helium gleaming under stars, and all I could summon was a single thought: *For now, goodbye.*

The beam of light hummed as I latched on.

To kill time on the journey, I practiced more jokes. *Why did the chicken cross the road?* Because he was genetically hardwired as an Earth creature to do so. *Knock-knock?* Who's there? *No one. Doors are a human construction and do not exist on other planets.* (Ha!)

It's unclear when things started to go wrong.

Perhaps it was when I began to sprout a tail.

I was four thousand miles above Earth's atmosphere, and there it was—crooked, with striped fur. I didn't have the ability to gasp; otherwise, I would have done so. A tail? Unless I was missing something dramatic about humans, that was incorrect. Quickly, I took in my surroundings, awareness hitting me with slow, terrible force: this wasn't the right route to Yellowstone. In my eagerness to perfect the knock-knock joke, I'd strayed off course, interacting with the wrong elements along the way. *Those* elements, mixed with Earth's atmosphere, would turn me into . . .

A cat.

I was a cat, crashing into North America. Faster, *faster*, landing paws-first in a tree. My claws dug into the branch beneath me, and immediately I coiled around, observing the zigzagged tail attached to my backside. It twitched—almost on its own—as if speaking to me. I could feel my paws tensing, the wind sifting through a large notch in my ear.

And what a sensation: to feel. To feel, finally. To have a body, even if it wasn't the one I expected. Yet my heart scrambled. Nothing in my studies had prepared me for this. Apart from a few anecdotes, I knew exceptionally little about cats. How could I live for a month as one?

On Earth, I had been very much looking forward to speaking words. I already knew what my favorite ones would be. *Tangerine*: so festive, rolling from the mouth. *Yellowstone*: a park that was home to bison and bears, forests and canyons. *Soul*: the beating in your body. Now I tested them with my throat—with my prickly tongue, horrible fangs poking into my lips—and only gurgling emerged.

The whole thing was entirely my fault. I knew this. *Never get distracted* is the first rule of space travel. But that didn't make it any less terrifying: to be alone in a tree, on a new planet, without knowing the language of cats. Was it even possible to communicate with humans this way? Did cats moo, or was that birds? There were all these new sensations, too—things I didn't expect to feel. The desire to spring from tree branch to tree branch, testing my balance. The way my ears were swiveling. The realization that if I saw an umbrella now, canopy flying open, I might actually be afraid of it.

Suddenly, the tree began to shiver with bursts of wind, and I arched my spine on instinct. *I have a spine*, I thought. A part of me was thrilled, while a bigger part yelled, *Storm!* A storm was coming. I contemplated lurching from the tree, but the ground looked soggy, like it would squelch beneath my toes. As a ranger, I would've worn boots, so I vowed to find some later, in whatever size was suitable for cats. Preferably leather boots. With some nice streaming shoelaces, and—

Oh! Scents began arriving from all directions: bitter smells, sweet smells. My nose sniffed the air, and I started peering around. The clouds were turning an alarming shade of plum. In my field of vision, I could see only sky, bushes, and a few tall grasses, swaying violently in the breeze.

My tail puffed with fear, which startled me even more. I didn't know that tails could puff. It seemed to say, *Where are we, exactly? And what happens now?*

Within fifteen minutes, rain began and refused to

stop. Flicking water off my ears did little good; the storm poured sideways, flattening my entire coat. *Can cats swim?* It was a pressing question, one I asked my tail. But my tail was ignoring me, hiding behind the curve of my legs. Something told me I might not like the answer anyway.

Around the base of the tree, dark water was rising.

And rising.

And—

I saw it in the distance then. The speck of a rowboat bobbing toward me. Through the thunderous rain, closer and closer she came: a tiny figure dressed in overalls, a yellow slicker, and boots three sizes too big. Her boat careened wildly in the floodwaters as she yelled words in my direction. They sounded like: "I'VE COME TO SHAVE YOU!"

Could this possibly be right? I wasn't immediately fond of my fur, but would *baldness* improve my look? The idea alarmed me. More alarming was the wind, which was picking up speed. Imagine you are on a new planet, experiencing gravity for the first time. Now imagine that hurricane-force winds are threatening to lift you into the sky. Balancing on that branch was almost impossible. I managed to steady myself just in time. Only seconds later, the tip of the human's boat slammed into the tree trunk. Everything shook. Bark split with a menacing *crack*, and the girl snapped her head up, eyes wide.

Despite the circumstances, I tried to savor this moment. It was my first time meeting a human; I didn't want to get it wrong. *Hello there* was the greeting I'd memorized—simple yet elegant—and I attempted this with a string of long, eager meows. It couldn't have gone worse. I sounded like a garbage disposal. (We will get to the evil of garbage disposals later. And seagulls! I must tell you about the seagulls.)

But now the girl was ordering me to jump.

"It's okay!" she shouted into the tree, her voice cutting through the wind. "I'm a Girl Scout, and I'm here to save you!"

Well, I'll admit that I was more than a little relieved. *Save* me, not shave me! Nevertheless, I squirmed. This small human was going to rescue me? She was maybe four and a half feet tall, and no more than eleven years old.

I hesitated, skidding back and forth on the branch, torn between options: stay in this tree, alone in a storm, or jump—with legs I barely trusted.

Stay or jump.

Stay or jump.

Stay or—

A sharp gust of wind decided for me, cracking the tree branch above my head. Instinct took over as my body pitched forward, away from the terrible *snap*.

I felt myself falling.

Then I felt myself questioning if I should have remained in the tree.

Because I'd misjudged the jump. The water was already swallowing me whole.

Here is an interesting fact. Being underwater is a little like floating in space. Except for the dull roar in my ears, there was barely any sound. Everything was dark, glittering, and lonely.

That doesn't mean I wasn't panicking.

I was panicking very much.

My legs flailed. My paws thrashed in front of me. Bubbles rose and popped in my throat.

You're immortal, I thought, trying to calm myself. *You cannot die, so this water won't harm you.* In a way, I was untouchable: my species has always existed in the universe and always will. But I'd never felt stress before—never understood the power of it. And embarrassment. I was ashamed to fail this spectacularly, after I'd longed for decades to be human.

Every traveler to Earth keeps a record: a series

of images captured, then shared with the rest of the hive. Over the years, I'd filtered through pictures of family Christmases, of dinners on New Year's Eve, of human birthday parties and picnics in parks filled with green. I had called up those images again and again—learning the humans' traditions, the lines of their faces. I wanted to try a cheese sandwich, too. I wanted to go to the movies. I wanted to walk with someone by a river on a blistering hot summer day.

All of this required being above water.

Luckily, the girl was already grabbing the scruff of my neck, yanking me from the deep. The air was a shock, maybe more so than the water, and I shook vigorously as she plopped me down. It was surprising, really: I found that I liked shaking, the way my body moved everywhere all at once. The boat shimmied beneath my paws.

"Oh my goodness!" the girl said, still shouting over the wind. "Are you okay?"

I thought very seriously about this question. Obviously, I was not. Cats and water don't mix. (I couldn't recall a great deal about cats, but I suspected this right away.) I liked that she asked, though, even if all I could answer was *mrrr*.

Here is something else: my chest crunched as I

looked at her. (Humans like the word *crunch*, and I believe I am using it properly here. You may correct me if I'm wrong.) Either way, glimpsing a human up close was something like a miracle. I was bowled over, entranced by the girl's tiny nose, her cheekbones so smooth under her light-brown skin. Yes, skin! With pores and everything.

I tried to memorize her at once, in case someone on my home planet wanted to know. Smallish ears. Roundish chin. Dimples.

Gripping the oars with white knuckles, the girl pushed hard against the rippling water, and I couldn't help but feel slightly powerless, tail curling around me in the frigid boat. My own skin prickled as objects floated by, trapped in the flood's current: a plastic Hula-Hoop, a deck chair, two inflatable lawn ornaments that looked suspiciously like gnomes.

It was all starting to hit me now—*really* hit me. The distance I'd traveled, the predicament I was in, the fact that I was *breathing* and couldn't quite figure out how. I inhaled harshly, too fast and too sharp; my lungs fluttered, causing me to wheeze, just as the boat careened dangerously to the left.

"I'm not really a Girl Scout anymore!" the human said suddenly, like she was purging a hair ball.

We will get to a discussion of hair balls. Oh, will we ever. But right then I just stared at her, unable to unravel how scouting played into this. Many areas of human life were still a mystery to me. I thought it best to give her a wise nod, like those that I'd witnessed on captured images of *I Love Lucy*, a human TV series that I especially enjoy. I tipped my head up and down.

The girl seemed mildly puzzled by this, her eyelashes fluttering.

But she rowed on.

Through the rain, I was beginning to see the shadowy outline of a house—a human house on stilts, with a wraparound porch. The lawn was fully submerged under a thick sheet of water. I sincerely hoped there was a plastic flamingo somewhere beneath the waves, to really give it that human touch.

As the boat shuddered, jerking us from side to side, a white-haired woman came into vision. She stood rigidly on the porch, a beach towel draped around her shoulders. Stocky and tough-looking, she was perhaps seventy in Earth years and seemed—in a human word—*furious*. I wondered if she could see me in the boat. Perhaps she was more of a dog lover. A bandanna was trembling around her neck, her light-brown skin glistening in the moonlight, and she was shouting something.

I'd worried about this, before my journey—how to follow human speech on Earth. Our species is so advanced, we have no use for words. We pass information telepathically; images float, are consumed, and that's it. Forget about chitchat. Forget about *How was your day?* (How I wanted someone to ask—to *care*—about my day!) So I'd studied whenever I could, revisiting scenes from *I Love Lucy* and picking up languages from previous travelers to Earth.

Now I was bombarded by sound, by *feeling*. It was both intensely wonderful and intensely distracting. I had to squint at the woman, trying to detect the subtle differences in her syllables. This was what I pieced together: a single word, over and over again.

Olive, Olive, Olive.

Either she was incredibly hungry, or this was raincoat girl's name.

Soon the boat thumped against the house's stairs, and the white-haired woman fled down the steps, her ankles steeped in water. She threw the towel off her shoulders; it was soggy in an instant, lugged away by the tide.

"Do you have any idea how *dangerous* that was?"

she yelled, grabbing the boat's stern and tying it quickly to the railing. That knot! It was ranger-worthy. "I've seen plenty of stupid antics in my day, but this one takes the cake."

I knew this wasn't the time to notice the older woman's wardrobe, but she was wearing a checkered shirt under a khaki vest—both with plenty of pockets. My whiskers twitched enviously. As a human, I would've liked to wear those clothes.

"Listen here, sailor," the woman continued, voice rumbly and slightly out of breath. "You could've bitten the dust out there. Am I making myself clear? Your mother didn't send you down here to disobey a direct order. So when I tell you not to go outside in a tropical storm, you have to listen to me."

It happened then: I felt myself being scooped into Olive's arms. She clutched me close to her chest, her raincoat quivering. I had no idea what to do. There were no drills for this, no training. In three hundred years, it had never occurred to me: *One day, a human girl will hold you.*

Was now an appropriate time to moo? Was I supposed to kiss her on both cheeks, as some people do? I went for a fail-safe option: going completely limp.

"I couldn't leave him there," Olive said, stepping

awkwardly from the boat to the steps, her rubber boots squishing in water. "I'm sorry, Norma. I just couldn't."

Norma towered above us, arms crossed, eyebrows knitted. I was slightly overwhelmed by the power of her presence—but also wanted to grab her face with my paws and shout, *Do you know how lucky you are to have eyebrows? Do you?*

When Norma spoke again, her voice was raspier. "You're not hurt anywhere, are ya?"

Olive shook her head.

"Well . . . good," Norma said, massaging a spot on her chest, as if her heart hurt. "Now, let's get inside, before this storm eats us up."

Then we were climbing the rickety steps. Norma unlatched the front door.

I felt myself shaking—this time, not from the cold.

I'd never heard of a mistake like this. No one in my entire species had *ever* ended up in the wrong body. It was supposed to go so smoothly: I would arrive on Earth as a human, interview for the park ranger position, accept the job immediately; my wilderness knowledge would astonish my colleagues. They'd throw a Welcome to Wyoming party in my honor, and I'd settle into a rented cabin, on the very edge of the woods, safe in the comfort of my plan.

But now? I was venturing even further into unknown territory.

"Don't be afraid, kitty," Olive said, slipping inside the house. She pushed off her raincoat hood, her hair wavy and dark, clamped down on both sides with daisy barrettes. A fellow flower enthusiast! We'd have so much to talk about, I thought, if I could talk. Did she know that flowers appeared 140 million years ago? Or that the largest flower on Earth is over nine feet tall?

Olive caressed my muzzle with a gentle hand. Maybe it was too soon to trust her, but there it was. A kernel of faith, blooming in my chest.

Carefully, she placed me on the ground, my paws touching floorboards for the first time. How many hours—how many *years*—had I spent imagining this moment? A human house! And me, inside it. Some things were exactly as I'd expected. There were books, magnificent books, stacked high against the living room walls. Wicker furniture dotted the space. And in the kitchen, I just knew there'd be a toaster. A *toaster*! Only humans could invent something so quaint. People cared deeply, about everything, even if it was just the crispness of their bread.

Other things about the house surprised me. For one, it was very quiet. In *I Love Lucy*, there were always noises. People laughing, making chocolate, a chorus of humans rushing in and out. Here, there was nothing but the howling of wind, the *squeak* of Olive's footsteps.

Norma trudged down a hallway and stamped back a moment later, a large stack of towels in her arms. "I've been listening to the radio, and they say the storm's getting worse. Some houses in Hilton Head are half underwater. Isle of Palms, too. Your mom's been trying to call, but the line won't stop dropping." Letting out a rough breath, she peered down at me. I could see all the way up her nostrils. "Now, I keep food around for strays—and I thought I knew about every cat in this neighborhood. Where'd you come from, huh?"

It was an excellent question. Unfortunately, I barely processed it. My brain was spinning out of control. *Hilton Head. The Isle of Palms.* I'd studied human maps, the gentle slope of lines across paper, and those places weren't near Yellowstone. No. Not at all.

The evidence was all around me: wicker furniture and baskets of seashells, beach towels and chunky sandals by the door. A plastic starfish was eyeing me from the wall. And the house—yes, the whole house—was on stilts. I can still remember the feeling of surprise and terror when I realized, *I am near the sea.* By any estimate, that put me at least two thousand miles away from my destination. At least two thousand miles from my pickup point, without any other way of returning home.

Theoretically, getting to this planet is the easy part. The real difficulty is traveling back. Atmospheric forces are much stronger on the way home—my energy alone isn't enough—so my entire species must pick me up. According to the schedule, the hive would arrive at precisely 9:01 a.m. on the twenty-first of July. My pickup point was incredibly specific: coordinates 44.4605 degrees north, 110.8281 degrees west—Yellowstone National Park.

If I wasn't there by the end of the month, if I missed the takeoff, I'd be stuck on Earth forever.

I gave myself a few moments to let that sink in.

Then I did what anyone would do in a fit of utter devastation. I began to destroy the curtains.

Maybe this is a good time to remind you: I had no idea how to be a cat. I was an actor without a script. If you were in my metaphorical shoes, could *you* avoid detection? Could you enter an alien world and fit in seamlessly? I was bound to fail in some respects, so please try not to judge me too harshly.

Even if you're acquainted with Earth, cats are easy to miss. They slink. They dash. They burrow in bushes, under couch cushions, in the bowels of handbags on closet shelves. I'll be honest and say that even the handsomest ones are comical to look at: ridiculously pointy ears, stringlike whiskers, and a constantly replenishing source of fur, which sticks to your tongue when you lick it. (Why would you want to lick it, you might ask? See my later discussion on keeping clean.)

Cats are considered a standoffish species, also

known as "aloof." Many prefer their own company, despise loud noises, and often stuff their bodies inside boxes for no apparent reason. Tuna fish is a yes. Garlic is a no. A group of them is called a *clowder*, not to be confused with *chowder*; there is no soup involved.

I wish I'd know any of this before I was required to play the part of a cat. I was forced to act purely on instinct.

And my instinct told me to destroy the curtains.

They were tan colored; I recall that very clearly. Soon my claws were buried inside the fabric, tugging at the cloth with swift pulls. I really did feel better as the thread unspooled beneath my paws. I liked the resistance, the feeling of battling something and winning. I liked controlling a small part of my fractured universe.

The woman called Norma shook the curtains, startling me. "Hey, hey, easy there, partner. I'm not a fan of these drapes, but I don't like ribbons, either. You're tearing them to shreds."

Olive reached down and scratched a spot behind my ears, which slowed my heart rate a little; it felt nice. All of a sudden, I also wanted her to rub my belly. Only for a second, only in the exact middle. But the feeling was definitely there.

"Do you think he's lost?" Olive asked. "Maybe some-one's missing him."

Norma considered this, then *tsk*ed. "He isn't the *best*-looking cat. That's not an excuse, absolutely not, but someone could've dumped him."

"How can people do that to animals?" Olive asked as wind battered the windows, shuddering the whole house. "Well, *I* think he's beautiful."

"I wouldn't go that far," Norma murmured.

Olive gazed into my eyes. "Either way, he has us. You hear that, kitty cat? We're here."

I was still having trouble breathing. Oxygen didn't agree with me nearly as well as helium, and my stress level was astronomical. Even so, Olive's words—the *us*, the *we*—wrapped around me, and I glimpsed something in that moment.

What it must feel like to have a friend.

If you watch any local news channel on Earth, you will discover the human-cat connection: humans have quite a history of rescuing cats from trees. Normally this is performed by a large person in a firefighter's suit, and the cat must be coaxed down with praise and the promise of crunchy treats. There is a big hoopla. I didn't realize, that first night, how much of a cliché I was—cold, hungry, yet pampered after my rescue.

Olive set up a space for me in her room, underneath a turtle night-light with an eerie green glow. I watched it suspiciously as she fluffed two blankets into a perfectly round cocoon. "That should do for now," she said, rising from her knees, and then dashing around the room. She was quick on her human feet and spoke the way a rubber ball bounces—with energy. "I know a whole lot about jaguars and snow leopards and

Chinese mountain cats, but not as much about house cats. I think I've done enough? You have water; you have food; I've set up a cardboard box and some newspaper in the bathroom. Am I missing anything?"

I had no idea. Absolutely none. At the same time, I did wonder: *Is it common for humans to speak with cats?* Nothing in my research strictly forbid it, but Olive's language and my language were not the same. How did she know I was following along? I couldn't tell her that I was; my vocal cords just weren't up to snuff. Despite my intelligence, speaking the language of people was pitifully beyond my reach.

She flicked off the lamp, the light from the green turtle washing over us. It gave me an uneasy feeling, but I still managed to crawl into my bedding, wrapping my tail comfortably around me. Outside, the wind was growing softer and softer. And I knew I was supposed to be drifting to sleep. That's what humans do: they sleep for a third of their lives. This is an enormous waste. How can they have all this—their fingers and their toasters and their movie theaters with plush seats—and just sleep right through it?

"Norma's my grandmother," Olive said a few moments later, pulling the sheets up to her chin. "I don't know if you could tell, but we're not that close.

My mom calls her 'the captain' because she used to run a shrimp boat—and she still calls everyone 'sailor.' Usually I only see her for Christmases and one week in the summer. But I'm . . . well, this year I'm here all summer."

I listened. What she was telling me, in those moments in the dark, seemed important.

I just didn't know why.

"The thing is," Olive said, her voice getting softer, "my dad died when I was really little—too young to remember him. And now my mom's got this new boy-friend, Frank. He's a life coach from California. They're traveling together until August, because he's giving all these speeches across America. Mom says it's better for me here, in Turtle Beach, so I can have a fun summer. But I can't help thinking that . . . that Frank just didn't want me around. He wants my mom to move with him to Sacramento, too. *Permanently*. Which means I'd have to start a new school and everything. We live in Maine now, which is a long way from California."

My throat clenched. I wasn't sure that I liked this "Frank," and dislike was new for me. Before that, the closest I'd come was my aversion to our neighbors, the Lalarians, who are fond of singing in shrill voices for months on end. Very loud, very distracting.

"Did you know that alpine swifts can fly six months without stopping? Sometimes I wish I could do that. Just . . . fly back home when I want to. Fly away when I need to." Her lip was quivering, but she bit it down. "Anyway, what should I call you? Maybe you already have a name, but it feels wrong to just call you 'kitty.' You deserve more than that." She spun over slowly, my night vision sharpening. I could make out all of her facial features as she peered down at me. There was a slight gap between her two front teeth.

"How about Leonard?" she asked. "You look like a Leonard, and that was my great-grandpa's name."

Half of me was thrilled, I'll admit—to be given a human name, a *family* name. It sounded distinguished, gentlemanly, like I should be wearing a top hat or, at the very least, something with feathers. But it also seemed scarily permanent. While I was Leonard the cat, I wasn't a human. While I was Leonard the cat, I was stuck exactly where I was.

I lay awake that night, focused on the length of my forelegs, of my paws. I didn't like the shape of myself, exactly. What was with these whiskers, sticking so dramatically from my cheeks? What was the *purpose* of this unsightly tail? It was also slightly uncomfortable to be squeezed into such a small frame. I'd expected more room for the energy of me to bob around; this was like a human wearing a shoe several sizes too tight. But overall, it really was an amazing thing, to have a body. This thing that moved on my command, that had fur, that encapsulated me. I'd always appreciated that human phrase: body and soul. *I love you, body and soul*, one person might say to another. Now I had both.

Still, I was incredibly restless.

Shouldn't I use this time wisely? Discover more about these humans—and where I'd landed?

So, I found myself wobbling into the kitchen at around two in the morning. I was still getting used to my legs—and to the enormous moon beaming in the inky sky. I sat by the kitchen chairs, transfixed for a moment or two, thinking about the twelve moons orbiting my home planet—how none of them were quite as brilliant as this.

Then I saw what I was looking for.

On the table, in a strip of moonlight: a stack of mail.

There are many methods of human communication. The most common, of course, is speaking with their mouths. Gestures are essential, too: knowing when, how, and in what situation to show your teeth, wave your hands, stomp your foot. What comes next is slightly trickier: instant messaging, emails, letters slipped into boxes by your front door. I knew to read the mail. How would I learn about this human family otherwise?

Jumping onto the kitchen table (I was quite the accomplished jumper), I perused the envelopes with my paws, inspecting the typewritten words. Nothing stood out to me, really—so I had to open them all.

I cannot express this clearly enough: there is a reason why cats do not unseal envelopes. It is a thankless, near-impossible task, requiring all four paws and most of your back muscles. How do you unstick the paper cleanly, without destroying what's inside? Well, you do not. Around me was a tattered mess. Only three letters remained, after I got the hang of rolling onto my back, wriggling, and slitting the sticky paper with paws in the air.

The first was an electricity bill, which sounded tremendously exciting. (I was fooled.)

The second was a packet of coupons for jumbo shrimp and other "sea delights." (Based on my first experience with water, there is nothing delightful about the sea.)

The third was already opened. It was on crisp, yellow stationery, and said this:

Greetings from California, the Golden State!

Dear Olive,

I'm missing you a whole lot. I tried to find a postcard with a California bobcat on it (I know you like them), but no luck. Frank and I will keep looking! He's working on a new seminar called "The Power of You: Harnessing the Good Stuff," so we've been pretty busy.

I hope that you and Norma are finding lots of exciting things to do, too. I really want you to have a fun summer, Olive. Your dad loved Turtle Beach when he was a kid, and I'm sure that you will as well. Have you gone with Norma to the aquarium yet? Are you taking lots of pictures?

Speak soon. Calling you is always the best part of my day.

Remember that I love you so much,
Mom

I refolded the letter and tried not to sulk there in the moonlight, debris by my paws. I would never have this—not even for a second. This humanness. This love.

Here is what I adore about *I Love Lucy*. No matter how much trouble Lucy gets into, Ethel is always there; Ricky is always there; Fred is always there. So no one ever feels like I did that night: odd, broken, and alone.

I missed my planet. I didn't think I would, but there was a sensation swarming inside me, a deep yearning for the comforts of home: views of crystal mountains, dips in helium rivers, the peace of everything. I was used to being expansive and limitless; now I was confined to this tiny body, unable to move beyond Earth. More importantly, I couldn't sense the hive all around me. At home, loneliness does not exist. And I never realized how comforting that community was, until I felt the terrible loss of it. Even the shrill songs of the Lalarians would've been welcome.

Earth was lonely—and tiring.

My eyelids were starting to twitch from exhaustion; my head began to fog. Taking the hint, I crawled to the floor, lay down, and told myself that I would only close my eyes for a second. Only a second, nothing more.

I dreamed. I didn't know it was possible for cats to dream, but there I was. A Yellowstone park ranger. Magnificent fingers. Ranger badge. Strolling through the wildflowers beneath a summer sky. When I woke up, my paws were flitting on the cold tile, and the radio was whispering in the background. *Thankfully*, it said, *South Carolina has missed the worst of the storm.*

South Carolina. So I was in South Carolina. I kept my eyes tightly shut, thinking. Reaching my pickup point was essential: the hive couldn't find me on Earth otherwise. But how could I travel from here to Yellowstone without money or hands or the ability to drive a car? Maybe I could—

Sniff!

Something sniffed. And then I began to notice a hot,

moist smell, inches from my nose. Flinging my eyes open, I lurched sideways into the air—a natural reaction, I assure you, because splayed out on the tile was a beast, camouflaged as a gigantic lump of fur.

No, not a beast? A dog. I could tell by the wetness of his black snout, and the way the tip of his tongue poked between his teeth. On Earth, dogs—not cats—are called "man's best friend." In those moments, I couldn't possibly see why. He was easily twenty times my size and had so much fur—white, fluffy—that I feared I'd get lost inside it if I ventured too close.

But closer I slunk, stepping toward him, my ears pinned back.

He'd yet to open his eyes.

When he did, he lifted one eyelid, then the other. Slowly. Purposefully. *You are here*, he told me with his pupils, which were watery and deep, like miniature universes. My heart stuttered, my spine beginning to arch—but I picked up his language instantly. The cadence of his breath. The mellow wag of his tail. How his eyes softened as he looked at me. Dogs, I've learned, are like my species: they say so much without saying anything at all.

Trying to swallow my fear, I took a final step and sniffed him in return. He had a very strong smell.

You are here, he repeated, moving nothing but his pupils. *There you are.*

As a human, I would've known exactly how to respond. I'd imagined the motion of saying hello to dogs—a quick scratch of the neck, a calm pat of the head. But somehow, patting his head as a cat seemed wrong. He was clearly waiting for a response, though, and I couldn't give myself away as an impostor, as the alien that I was.

So I let out a kind meow, almost a *mrrrrr*—something of my own creation. He appeared pleased with this, because suddenly he lumbered up, dragging his tongue over the crest of my face. Correct me if I'm wrong, but none of you've had firsthand experience with this particular dog's tongue. What you must understand is: he has a very significant tongue, full of saliva. My fur spiked. My nose scrunched, causing me to sneeze repeatedly.

At least I wouldn't need a bath on Earth.

He inched back, admiring his work, sunlight dancing around his paws. Then he told me, in a series of friendly snorts, that he would keep my secret. I followed his eyes up to the table, where a dozen envelopes lay in plumes of confetti. So he'd seen me destroy the letters. And perhaps he knew—that I was not of this Earth.

We'll blame the letters on the birds, he said, woofing once. He motioned with this nose to the bright windows. *The birds.*

I hadn't the faintest clue what he was talking about. But he had such confidence in this idea that I went with it.

I decided to test the waters even further, offering a friendly joke.

Knock-knock, I said, imitating his harmonic woof, scrounging in my belly for the sound. A "woof" wasn't out of reach for me like human language was, but what I produced wasn't exactly right. I attempted it again, experimenting with a bit more vibration, then throwing in a few tail wags for good measure.

His ears perked. *The door? Is someone at the door?*

No, I said, more pleased with my dog noise this time. *It was a joke.*

I did not hear the doorbell. At the doorbell, I will bark.

I fanned my whiskers, softening my eyes. *You must say, "Who's there?"*

You know who is at the door? Intruder? Friend?

Well. Never mind.

Backing slightly away from him, I stretched. Stiffness ran through my limbs. One downside of having a body is that it can fail you. Sometimes you wake up and there are aches where there were no aches before. Feeling untidy, I started licking the white fur of my bib. The licking was a surprise to me, and I pulled back, hair on my tongue, startled. What was happening to me?

I tried not to dwell on it for too long.

Outside was the shrill call of seagulls, the sweet slap of waves. Hopping onto the windowsill, I could see that the floodwaters had receded. Everything was a flat plane of green and blue: marsh grass and trees, followed by a thin strip of ocean. I'd never viewed the ocean this close. From my galaxy, Earth is a pinprick, and water is just a color: not a moving, breathing, living thing. Not something to be painted and studied and waded in; you cannot dip your toes in a color, especially when you have no toes.

"Leonard? Leonard, where'd you go?"

Olive's worried voice trailed through the house, and another new feeling invaded me: guilt. I felt guilty for leaving her, for slinking off in the middle of the night without saying where I was going. I called out to her with my voice, wishing I could speak words like *In the kitchen! Right here!* In return, the dog barked a mighty *woof* that was full-throated and admirable, and Olive was able to find me by the refrigerator.

"I see you've met Stanley," she said, smiling a bit. "I think you're going to be friends."

I assumed that Stanley was the dog and not the refrigerator, but I made a mental note to check his collar later, just in case. Olive crouched down, petting the back of my neck. I'll confess that I leaned in, just slightly. An early morning scratch is often the best kind.

A few minutes later, we crowded into the living room to eat breakfast, the little TV flickering on. The screen showed a small amount of wreckage from the storm—shingles flying, porches damaged—which seemed logical. More puzzling were the commercials. I'd seen several back on my home planet, but they were mystifying things. From what I was able to piece together, commercials were a sort of guidebook for humanity. They told you what salad dressing to buy, what mattress to sleep on, what type of medicine to consume. As a human, you should like your food "fast." You should maintain a muscular physique. You should enjoy ball sports, play them frequently, and look forward to a time when you do absolutely nothing but golf. There was so much *should*, so much that made no sense.

Like everything on this planet, it was overwhelming.

I missed the straightforwardness of home: We are

always calm. We notice the world. There is comfort in the beauty and peacefulness of our planet.

Still, I tried to focus on Earth's positive qualities, the things I'd yearned for in my galaxy. An example: food. In this house, cereal was clearly highly important. Flakes don't have the same appeal as cheese sandwiches (few meals do), but that first morning I was blinded by the variety: Coco Pops! Froot Loops! Cinnamon Toast Crunch! All in bright, colorful boxes. On the couch, Olive and Norma ate their cereal with metal spoons, exchanging words with each other.

"I'll be honest with you, sailor," Norma said to Olive, loosening the bandanna around her neck. "I'm out of practice with the 'caretaker' thing. Here's what I do know: how to run a tight ship. That's what we're going to do this summer. Run on routine—like the tides. So we should start thinking about activities, things to schedule in. You like motorcycles?"

"Um . . ." Olive said, sheepish.

"Scratch that. I've got this motorcycle I'm fixing up—the sidecar still needs work—but I'll put that on hold. What were you going to do this summer?" Norma drummed her fingers on her knees. "You know, before your mom and Frank decided to have you spend some time here."

"Well," Olive said, a hint of sadness seeping through, "my friend Hazel's family owns a farm. They'd said I could help out with the horses and the goats and stuff. Did you know that each baby goat has a unique call, like a name?"

"No goats in Turtle Beach, I'm afraid. What we do have is marine life—an aquarium and an ocean full of it. We could also set up some good old-fashioned arts and crafts."

From my position on the rug, I studied them—these people. Norma was stiff, rugged, like the core of an exoplanet. And Olive was a ball of energy, like a dwarf star. As she chewed, her feet moved to a soundless beat, and her eyes blinked sharply. Call it my hyper-intelligence, call it one species recognizing another, but I had the distinct sense that Olive was smart. Incredibly smart. Something about the way she carried herself, the way she *observed.*

"You haven't touched your crunchies," she said to me after finishing her cereal. A frown creased her forehead. "You're not hungry?"

Oh, I was. There was a grumbling, rumbling sensation in the pit of my stomach. I'd been trying to ignore it, because if anything was going to signal *this cat is not a cat*, it would be this: I had no idea how to consume food. Even as I watched Olive's jaw work, I couldn't quite figure out the mechanics. I'd assumed that I'd have time to practice, as a Yellowstone ranger, in the privacy of my own cabin.

But I hadn't eaten anything since my arrival to Earth. A hungry cat—a *normal* cat—would eat. So I had to think quickly, as she placed the bowl of crunchies in front of me. *How* would a cat eat? Surely not like humans, with delicate bites and dainty fingers. Did cats use silverware? Miniature silverware?

Claws, fangs—these terrible things I had. These I would use.

I pawed at the kibble, stalling for time. Then I just hoped for the best, opening my mouth as far as it would go, lowering my head to the dish, and filling my entire mouth with crunchies. This was my first mistake. Mouths should not be entirely filled.

I couldn't chew. I could barely breathe. Gagging, I spat out some of the kibble, sprinkling the rug with dull *plop*s.

Olive patted me on the back. "You okay, Leonard?"

"Leonard?" Norma asked.

"Doesn't he look like a Leonard?"

Norma cocked her head as she watched me. My cheeks were still packed full of kibble.

"I don't see it."

Eventually I clamped down with my teeth, willing my jaw to work. I learned how to maneuver my throat, how to produce the exact right amount of saliva without spilling it abundantly from my mouth. And all the while, Olive was there.

Perhaps I'm wrong, but I got the impression that she was cheering me on.

There is a debate in our galaxy over whether or not we have souls. I believe we do. I believe we always have. Perhaps we've just allowed ourselves to forget.

A famous human once wrote that "the soul travels," that the universe is just a "road for traveling souls." I couldn't have explained it any better myself, except maybe to add this: Other travelers make the journey worthwhile. People like Olive, who petted my neck in a careful way. Who asked if I preferred wet food or dry, and would I like some extra cushions for my bed upstairs.

So, while I was in an incredibly difficult position, homesick and trapped and struggling with my kibble, a part of me did acknowledge that I was lucky to have landed here. Olive didn't even yell at me when she noticed the shredded envelopes. She just sifted through the wreckage and declared, "We *definitely* need to get you a scratching post."

Stanley added, very helpfully, *It was the birds.*

I was still in the kitchen when Norma spoke on the telephone, then abruptly ended the call. "Something's happened at the aquarium," she rasped to Olive, rolling up her plaid shirtsleeves. "Chop-chop, sailor. You're coming with me. I've got to get the computers fired up, find some records for the Save the Sea Turtles event . . ."

My mind caught on "computer." I knew that word. Computers are all-powerful sources of information, relied upon by humans for a variety of messages and data. You can hardly exist on Earth without one. Maybe it would provide some guidance on how to get to Yellowstone, when all I had were paws.

"My truck's in the shop," Norma said to Olive. "Let's see if the bus is running after the storm. Go ahead and grab your backpack, too. It could be a while. Take something to keep you busy."

This was when I had an idea. Or maybe it was Stanley who tipped me off, his tail thwacking the edge of Olive's backpack. The bag was quite large for her size; it had wide pockets and was shaped like a turtle's shell. The middle was half unzipped—open and waiting.

Now, I must say that I am not a small cat by any means. While my forelegs are slim, my stomach neatly tucked, there's a good stretch to me. I could drape over someone's shoulders and dangle like a scarf. So, stuffing myself into that backpack was a challenge. Stanley watched—without helping, I might add—as I waddled and wiggled, contorting my way into the darkness of the bag. Inside, everything was muffled and hot and cramped.

Stanley sniffed around me. *You smell worried.*

I am, I admitted, giving him a doglike whimper.

You should howl. You will feel better if you a-woo.

My whiskers softened. *Do cats howl?*

I will teach you, he said.

Seconds later, footsteps.

I felt the backpack lifting, heard Norma saying, "What've you got in here, anchors?"

And Olive replied, as they headed out the door, "Just some books about animals."

The trick was to stay incredibly still, storing all the air in my chest. How long could cats hold their breath? I swayed in that bag, my paws tightly tucked, my body folding in ways I didn't expect. Tail over head. Legs on back. Each of Norma's footsteps jolted through my core. But I think it would've been all right, if not for the bus.

You see, public buses have a very specific scent, a highly penetrating odor that seeps into your pores; you can't wash it off, even with extra-bubbly soap. As a stowaway, I was extremely nervous to begin with, but my anxiety spiked when—through a hole in the fabric—I saw that the bus was full of all kinds of humans. People with mustaches. People with blue hair. People licking frozen sticks, and sharing music in small pods, and bobbing their heads as they spoke with each other. Frustration and excitement battled in my belly; it was the most I'd ever interacted with humanity—and I was stuck in a backpack.

A hot backpack. A backpack growing hotter. I could hardly stand it.

Olive said, "Do you have any stingrays at the aquarium?"

Norma said, "We've got three."

And I said, *Mrrrrrrrr-meow-rrraaar*, clawing my way out of the bag, springing into the stale air. I floated there for a startling second—and wondered, very briefly, if cats could fly. But no. The floor was tacky where I landed, coated with bits and pieces of discarded gum. Summer sun pelted my spine as I crouched low, humans glaring down at me. Some even screamed. Of course they did, with such a wild entrance.

I do wonder if I was conforming to some ridiculous stereotype of aliens: that we burst from fog or rise viciously from the sea. That we descend from clouds on otherwise perfect days, wreaking havoc on the landscape. Alien films, I've learned, depend heavily on this arrival—a moment of extraordinary surprise, when a creature from another universe appears with both shock and horror.

This was not how I'd imagined my first contact with a large group of people. There were no dinner forks. No crystal chandeliers. I was an outsider, unable to present a knock-knock joke, striped fur ruffling as humans clutched their chests and snickered. My heart thumped in my rib cage.

"Leonard!" Olive gasped, reaching down to scoop me up. "How'd you even get in here?"

We all lurched forward then, the bus driver slamming on the brakes and yelling from the front seat, "Please tell me that isn't a *cat*!"

What other animal could I be? I suppose, if my fur was fluffed enough, I might pass for a bear (a rather small, catlike bear). Perhaps even a young tiger, in the right lighting, from a far distance away. Alas, I could not deny the pads of my paws or the sharp points of my ears, so we were told to leave the bus immediately—Olive, Norma, and I. We watched it spurt and gurgle away, sloshing through storm puddles, everything glistening under a thin haze of dew.

It was Olive who eventually broke the silence, her shoes scuffing the sidewalk. "I don't understand how he even managed to get in there. It's amazing."

Norma appeared both impressed and displeased. "Amazing is one word for it."

"Do you . . ." Olive said, pausing in the middle. She was still cradling me in her arms. "Do you think that I could maybe keep him? Really keep him? If we put up flyers and no one says he's theirs?"

Norma scratched the back of her neck, just underneath the bandanna, her vest gleaming in the heat. "I don't think that's such a good idea, sailor. It's a big responsibility. *Huge.* How does Frank feel about cats?"

Olive widened her eyes. "I can't just turn Leonard over to the shelter. I know what happens to a lot of cats at shelters. *Please?* I promise that I'll take care of him all by myself. We won't bother you at all."

Norma softened a bit, blowing air from her lips. "I can't promise anything. But how about we bring Leonard to the vet, get him all checked out? Take things from there."

The sky was simmering then, a brilliant shade of blue. My shadow interlocked with Olive's on the sidewalk.

"Okay," Olive said, satisfied for the moment. "Are we heading back to the house?"

"Heck no," Norma said. "We've got to keep this show on the road. The aquarium's not too far. You mind walking a bit? I can take Leonard, if he's weighing you down."

"No thanks," Olive said. "I'm good." She held me closer still, and I found—to my surprise—that I didn't mind at all.

Perhaps I should explain the consequences of one of my species being discovered by a human. Say you've taken on the form of a walrus and are living in a remote pod of mammals in the Arctic. You've gotten the hang of your flippers; you are able to expertly wield your tusks, skillfully twitch your whiskers. But suddenly an explorer visits your part of the world and witnesses—through the night vision of his expensive camera—that instead of snoozing with the other walruses, you are waddling to the beach every evening, scrawling complex mathematical equations in the sand.

What, then?

Never trust a human. That's what my species believes. We are warned very clearly before our departure to Earth about maintaining the secret, about the consequences of saying, *I am not like you.* I've heard this argument so many times before: that revealing ourselves would place our entire planet at risk. Wouldn't the humans—*especially* the humans—try to invade us, colonize us, change everything that we are?

By now, you might have figured it out: that I believe in the goodness of people. That I was willing to give up anything and everything to become one, even for a month. Even for a day. Of course, there was a chance that humans would visit us, disrupting our lives of logic and harmony—but I still remember staring at a dark horizon and *wishing* that humans would come.

Maybe someone, then, would care about my day.

A man named Q met us at the aquarium door, and
at first I didn't identify him as human. He was wearing a foam fish head, an enormous backpack, and a
shirt with a variety of palm trees. A Hawaiian shirt,
I've come to understand—the king of shirts. If I could
wear any item of clothing, it would be from Hawaii.
For a second I was envious of him: how he so easily
extended his hand to Olive, greeting her in way that I
never could.

"You must be Olive the granddaughter. I'm an old
friend of Norma's," Q said, tipping his fish hat, then
peering down at me. His skin was white, and his
eyes, I would later realize, were the same color as the
aquarium tanks. "And who's this? My new boss?"

Olive giggled—the first time I'd heard a human
laugh outside of a television program. The noise

unraveled me slightly; I didn't know anything could sound like that. Like lightness itself.

"This," Olive said, "is Leonard."

Q sized me up. "Nice-lookin' cat," he finally said, which I knew was factually untrue. Hadn't he noticed the notch in my ear? The way my tail bent to the side? Thankfully he made no comment about letting a cat into an aquarium. What he did was open the door.

Inside, the walls glittered. A colossal model stingray shimmered from the rafters. I had never pictured an aquarium—had no episode of *I Love Lucy* to guide me—so each curve of the wall, each bend of the path, felt like landing on an alien planet all over again. Everything was brilliant and quiet and blue, tanks lit up in the near darkness. And so many fish! Gigantic fish! Miniature fish! Fish with golden fins, swishing tails, stripes down their backs. When Olive set me down, I froze on the rubber floor, in the halo of a penguin footprint, absolutely in awe of life on Earth.

Norma volunteered to take Olive to the office, but Q said, "Nah, let her stick with me." So we followed him. Olive hooked her hands into the pockets of her overalls and gazed with big eyes at the tanks, watching the fish dart. I saw something of myself in her, the way she was taking in her environment, full of wonder.

"You know," Q said, clapping his hands together, "Turtle Beach Aquarium is older than the town itself." I think he got the distinct sense that Olive and I needed to be entertained—that otherwise we'd be wandering alone through the shark tunnels, through the Underwater Explorer Passageway, where jellyfish plumed in the dark.

Despite my focus on accessing a spare computer, I found myself—quite against my will—wrapped up in the mystery and amazement of it all. Q spoke with such gusto, as I'd hoped to on Earth. His life was the human existence I'd wanted for myself.

"When the first settlers came to Turtle Beach, they said, we don't need no stinkin' banks, no stinkin' grocery stores—all we need is an aquarium that is just the right amount of cheesy. With plenty of whirly thingamabobs on the walls for the tourists. There also must be ice cream, of exactly two flavors, and this place must exist forever, even in the event of an apocalypse."

Olive blinked, a smile curling on her lips. "Is any of that true?"

Removing his fish hat, Q clucked his tongue. "Hard to say. Sometimes we have *three* different kinds of ice cream. Don't try the clam flavor. Bad clams, man." He swept his brownish hair back with one hand. "Joking aside, we do a lot of good here. Most of these fellas have been rescued from one place or another: fishing nets, washed up on the coast, injured by boats. Some of them we can rehabilitate; others will just have to stay a while longer, but we sure are lucky to have them around."

Trailing along the illuminated path of penguin footprints, we curved into a tunnel, glass arching over our heads. Light and dark swirled in patches. Rotating my ears, I looked up to see two enormous creatures, circling with swift strokes of their tails.

"That's Steve," Q said. "And that's Martin. You afraid of sharks?"

Olive shook her head. "Not really."

"Good. Seriously misunderstood creatures, sharks. If humans want to step inside *their* ocean, we should be prepared to accept the consequences. But hey, that's just me. See those little guys, right there? The nurse sharks. They're friendly." He paused. "So tell me about your cat. We don't get many cats in here."

Olive said, "I'm not sure if he's my cat yet."

"I see, I see. Well, he looks like a good friend to have."

My chest puffed a little with pride. I'd always hoped

for the opportunity to be a friend—to *have* a friend. Even here, in the aquarium, I was mildly scared of the water: about the possibility of the tanks bursting, of somehow finding myself submerged. But another thought came, strangely, right after the fear: *Olive will protect me.*

"You know," Q continued, "we could use an extra set of hands this summer, especially with the big Save the Sea Turtles event coming up. That is, if you're interested. Your grandmother said you'd be here until August."

Olive squirmed. "I think I'm supposed to do arts and crafts."

"You can make a pipe-cleaner octopus. How 'bout that?" There was a pause. "Truth is, I do a little bit of everything around here, and it wouldn't hurt to have someone else around, help me feed the fish, clean a few tanks."

"Okay. But I'm . . . I'm not . . ." Olive blew out a breath. "Frank says I'm not very good at talking to people."

Q frowned. "Who's this Frank, then?"

"My mom's boyfriend. He's a life coach, which I guess means he tells people what to do with their lives. Anyway, I like talking about animals—a *lot*. I know loads about them: marine iguanas, white tigers, you name it. Sometimes it feels like I've memorized so many facts that I might explode if I don't tell someone. Sometimes I blurt them out at people. And then . . . well, I guess not everyone wants to hear about iguanas. Or naked mole rats. Or mouse deer. I don't want to say the wrong things."

Q thought about this for a long moment. "I happen to believe you're a great conversationalist. And here it doesn't really matter how you are with people. How are you with *fish*? Okay, okay. I've got an idea." We scooted over to the next tank, where a school of butterfly fish bobbed in the fluorescent light. "That's Cletus and Octavia and Kim. They're very conversational, so don't let them talk your ear off. Just say, Cletus, I ain't got the time . . . What's that?" Q cupped his hand to his ear, pressed both to the tank. "Mmm-hmm, yep. Yes, I see. And then what?"

We waited as the fish spoke.

I had no idea that some humans could speak to fish.

"Well," Q said, pulling back from the tank. "That settles it. Octavia said that you rock. I told her, 'Kids don't say *rock* anymore, Octavia,' but she just wouldn't hear it. So you in?"

I didn't hear Olive's answer. Because at that exact moment, as I was trying to get a better look at the fish, I bopped my nose on the glass. It wasn't a gentle bop, either—more like a smash. And it hurt; my nose was lightly throbbing.

"Ouch," Olive said, like she could feel it, too. "You okay, Leonard?"

No. No, I wasn't. I could feel pain—not just discomfort or stress, but real, actual *pain*. Perhaps you can imagine the growing sense of panic that rushed through my chest. Why hadn't I considered it before? Everything had gone disastrously wrong with my transformation, so why not this, too? My immortality should have stayed with me, despite my earthly shell. On this planet, I was supposed to feel everything, *except* physical pain. Pain meant decay. Pain meant fear. Pain meant mortality.

Before my trip to Earth, I'd memorized a variety of human expressions and felt prepared to whip them out at a moment's notice. *Don't cry over spilt milk. I have bigger fish to fry. Curiosity killed the cat.* Now the last one took on new meaning.

It felt like a warning.

In this body, on this planet, I was just as vulnerable as anyone else.

Are you still listening? Can you hear me?

I hope so. The next part is very important.

10

I couldn't eat the crackers. We were in the staff lounge, crowded around the table with a package of saltines—which were salty, as their name suggested— and I couldn't eat them. I couldn't eat them because I was a cat, and if I did, the salt would crystallize in my bladder, forming a harsh chemical block, and I would be unable to urinate for many days. Apparently this was extremely painful. All of this was told to me by Q, who sat munching the saltines, his arms slung over the back of his chair.

I'd forgotten about the computer and was trying to focus on small things. How the staff lounge smelled: soggy, musty. Noises in the background: tanks sloshing, Olive pressing the buttons of a vending machine. But realization kept pounding me like winds in a storm. I wasn't sure that I could feel my whiskers; everything seemed suddenly blurry.

Mortal. I was mortal. I could die on this planet—die at any moment, from anything.

"Did you know your cat's kind of cross-eyed?" Q said to Olive, mouth half full. "It's like he's thinking real hard and his eyes have just—*boop!*—gone inward."

"I wonder what he thinks about," Olive said, plopping down with a can of lemonade.

"Oh, I know. How strange humans are. That's what they're all thinking," Q said, gesturing behind him to the fish. "You ever wonder why we *skateboard*? Have *pie-eating* contests? My cousin Bernie, he just bought his kid one of those whatchamacallits? Those stuffed animal horses on a stick. Calls it Mr. Stickhorse. Has a theme song for it and everything: *Come on, Mr. Stickhorse, give me a smile!* Song needs a little work, if you ask me."

Olive took a sip of lemonade. "Rubber ducks. That's another thing."

"See!" Q said, slapping the table. "Proving my point. Humanity is a strange, strange beast, my friend."

Wrapping my tail tightly around my body, I was listening but not listening—seeing but not seeing.

I could feel the bones inside me. I could feel myself growing older, second by earthly second.

Norma trudged into the room at that moment, telling us that she'd updated the records and prepped food for the African penguins. "I thought we had a bunch of flooding in the sea lion center," she said, "but it could've been a lot worse."

Could it? I wasn't sure.

You might say that I was half in denial as we swept out of the aquarium and into Q's car; it was bright red with silver wingtips that sparkled in the sun and looked very much like a spaceship, if you believe any of the movies. "It's a classic," Q said. "And by classic, I mean it's old, but tell me, tell me *honestly*, if you've ever seen a car this cool."

I had barely seen any vehicles at all.

The interior was rather impressive: soft leather and windows that, when cracked, let in a briny breeze. We cruised down crowded streets as Olive tucked me to her chest, and I tried to narrow my gaze—focusing on her daisy barrettes, on flowers, on good things in the world. Norma suggested that we should purchase a cat carrier (if "traveling with Leonard" was going to be a daily activity), but my heart was beating too fast to fully process this.

I just wanted to stay alive.

"Hey," Olive said, rubbing her dry nose against my wet one, "it's okay. It's only a car. We'll be there soon."

For a brief flash, I desperately wanted to believe that I was just a regular cat—afraid of cars or the breeze or travel—and I could be comforted by my human's nose, by a soothing whisper in my ear. But my universe was imploding, and Olive didn't even know it. I had no way to tell her, no way to make her understand.

"His heart's beating really fast," Olive said.

"'Course it is," Norma said. "Cats hate riding in the car. He should be—"

"No, I mean *really* fast," she said. "And he's drooling a lot."

Norma swung around in the front seat just as my eyes began to roll into the back of my head. Eighteen hours after learning to breathe, I was hyperventilating, my chest rising and falling in rapid bursts. It did occur to me, as Q pressed the gas pedal, as Olive's heartbeat sped to match my own, that I was in trouble. Earthly trouble. Here was another downside of having a body: sometimes you lose control.

11

Dolphins should be running the world. As much as I appreciate humanity, it's obvious that dolphins are the most intelligent creatures on Earth. (Can you imagine humans thriving so well under the sea, using echolocation and swallowing fish whole?) Given this, I've come to believe that veterinarians exist for two purposes: first, to treat the sick and the injured, and second, so that humans can keep a watchful eye on every species, so none—such as the hyper-intelligent dolphin—can rise above them.

No one seems particularly worried about a cat takeover. I am unsurprised. Arriving at Turtle Beach Veterinary Clinic, my bib was slick with drool, and I looked very much the alien I was: spiky, wide-eyed, and shivering. Quiet mews vibrated my rib cage. Q wrapped me in a bright green beach towel.

"He was fine," Olive whispered. "He was fine and then . . ."

And then everything was startlingly black. Piecing it together after the fact, I understand that my eyes closed in Olive's arms, that my body went limp, and for a few moments, I wasn't anything. I did not exist.

Johnny Cash woke me up. There were bright lights in the examination room, sharp smells, and Johnny Cash playing quietly on the intercom: a gravelly song about walking a line. You may have heard of this particular phrase: that someone is "going through a lot." As if "a lot" is a direction, something to pass over, like wading through water. This is what I remember. I remember the song—and a pair of humans hovering over me, poking and prodding this new body of mine. Swatting them away was useless, even with my claws out. My reaction time was slow, my vision foggy.

"He's pretty young, judging by his teeth," the vet said. "Maybe two, three years old. You say you just adopted him?"

"Yes," Olive said, at the same time Norma added, "Not quite."

The examination table was silver. The wallpaper was striped. A handwritten sign told us THE DOCTOR IS IN. And I lay there, blinking slowly, as the vet threw around words like *microchip, vaccinations,* and *panic attack.*

I have blocked out so much of what happened next, but I recall thinking a great deal about immortality. On Earth, I was vulnerable. On Earth, everything was temporary. The average human lives 28,835 days, a staggeringly small number. It's only 5,475 days for cats.

"But he'll be okay," Olive asked, strain in her voice. "Right?"

The vet said I needed rest. I needed calm. As a rescue, I was "going through a lot."

That night, I opened my eyes to see particles shifting above me. And for a moment, I thought I saw an infinite wilderness of stars. I thought I was on my planet—safe, wrapped in the numbness of calm. But it was just a trick of the light, just a bit of dust, nothing like home.

No one talks to cats about immortality. No one
questions dogs about the shortness of their existence. But humans, they are always wondering what
it might be like, to live and live and _live_. I understand this now—where they're coming from. After
the vet, I was paralyzed with fear in the beach house,
afraid to move from my fluffed blankets. Every noise
slicked back my ears. What would happen if the walls
abruptly collapsed? If I slipped on a banana peel, as
human cartoons so often suggest?

It's not like I had days to waste. At the end of the
month, I would either make it to Yellowstone or remain
stuck as a cat—without hands, without the hive, and,
most importantly, without my immortal life. For the
record, cats do not have nine lives—only one—and I
should have spent this one traveling. I should've been

searching for bus routes, plane tickets, waterways of the Carolinas. Anything to get me out.

Instead I sat. And I shook. And I watched Home and Garden Television for the entire next day, listening to Olive tell me about the animals in the marsh: mice and mud crabs, spoonbills and white shrimp. "You have to watch out for the gators," she said, and it struck me that life on Earth could look extremely alien, with large teeth and green scales. And humans were scared of extraterrestrials? Of *us*?

In that time, I also learned how to use a litter box, after sifting through pellets with my back paws, giving the impression that I knew exactly what I was doing.

But I was petrified. That should be said. I was deeply petrified: by sounds, by movements, by every jolt of the wind. I was even careful in this new litter box of mine, the safest of places, where I should've felt most secure—surrounded by nothing but the soothing scent of pine.

We watched *E.T.* that night. I like to think of this as fate, and not the whimsy of Monday evening broadcasting. After dinner, Stanley heaped himself on the linen rug, while Norma and Olive curled in matching armchairs. And I, well, I couldn't decide if I should stay in the room. When Olive introduced *E.T.* as "an alien film," my ears flattened. Would she draw the connection between this creature and me, if the idea was right in front of her?

In the end I decided to stay, because E.T. the extra-terrestrial appears nothing as I do. No fur, no tail. Was it startling to see an impression of aliens on Earth, bulb-headed and spiky fingered? Sure. But they did get my love of flowers exactly right. When E.T. revived the dead chrysanthemums, my tail twitched excitedly against the rug. I was so absorbed that, for a split second, I even forgot about my mortality. Olive knew most of the film's lines, mouthing along with the words, and I kept peering between her and the movie, as E.T. levitated balls in a bright room—showing the humans his planetary system, his world.

Just then, Olive glanced down at me, a hint of a smile on her face.

And it struck me that maybe I should smile back.

Person-to-person interaction depends on knowing when to smile. It's about waiting until the *exact* right moment and unleashing the appropriate grin. There are so many variables. Do you smile with or without teeth? How much should your lips stretch? And how do you recover, if you get it wrong?

So, from a safe position on the rug, I gazed up at

Olive, stretching my lips as far as they would go. Something told me I was missing the mark; it felt strange to expose my teeth so flamboyantly to the air. And Olive was leaning closer, tilting her head to the side.

"Are you okay, Leonard?"

I'm disturbed by how simpleminded I was. Cats rotate their ears, vibrate their tails, rattle their chests; they do *not* smile.

Olive stared at me for a good minute, a searching look in her eyes. If Norma hadn't asked if she wanted popcorn, calling her into the kitchen, I'm not sure what would have happened. Would she have confronted me? Asked more questions?

Are you really *okay, Leonard?*

Leonard, what are you?

13

I had to be more careful, more catlike. So, after the movie, I ate my kibble with caution, selecting one piece at a time. *See!* my every bite shouted. *I am convincingly feline! I am real!*

The rest of the evening, I lumbered around in a sort of dazed panic, overthinking every step I took. Would a cat be more graceful? Jump more? Meow with greater frequency? And how could I evade danger—slippery patches on the tile, pollen lurking in the air? Despite my exhaustion, I stayed up quite late that night, mulling over how I could avoid detection, travel to Yellowstone, and (quite importantly) remain alive.

My homesickness was only increasing. Earth had all this *oxygen*, but where was the helium? Where was the pale peach of helium clouds, the blue neon of helium rivers? I longed for the mellow *swoosh* of it. I longed for the nights when I'd hover at the edge of a crystal mountain, watching the stars dip and collide. There, I didn't have to worry—because worry did not exist.

I was still getting used to the unsettling feeling of being alone. Bodies can be useful, but they're also a barrier. Earth had so many barriers. And I missed the comfort of knowing that the hive was *there*, always there—a part of me as I was a part of them. All of us together, never lonely.

"I've never had a pet before," Olive said, breaking my thoughts just after midnight. In the darkness, I was curled at the foot of her mattress, my paws tucked under my chest; I found that I actually enjoyed a higher position, rather than slinking under her bed. It felt safer that way.

To my surprise, Olive switched on the lamp and gazed at me. "I'm not sure if I'm doing it right, this whole 'pet owner' thing. I don't even like the word 'owner.' You belong to yourself. Did you know that, pound for pound, the house cat is one of the fiercest animals alive? They're perfectly designed to hunt—and really, *really* good at it. Ancient Egyptians even worshipped them. There were cat gods and everything."

I blinked slowly, my eyes adjusting to the light.

"Which makes sense," she continued, sitting up. "The fierce thing. I think you're pretty brave, living in a new place and all. You could be really feisty or mean if you wanted to be, but you aren't like most cats, are you?"

My pupils dilated. Did Olive know? Had I given myself away with that smile?

"I can tell you're super smart. Maybe the smartest cat I've ever met. It's the eye-contact thing, like you're *actually* listening. And it's nice to have someone listen and not, you know, judge you." She paused, elbows on her knees. "Maybe you can promise me something."

I wasn't sure. Honestly, I was confused. What could I promise to her that would mean anything at all?

"Just . . ." she said, chewing her bottom lip. "Just don't think I'm weird like some people do. So here are a few things that you should know about me up front: I like overalls. They're comfortable and they have big pockets, which are useful. Especially if you're carrying treats for animals. I love animals a whole lot. One of the things I know about my dad is that he did, too. So I've collected all of these facts about them—and I like sharing them with people. Did you know that the milk of a hippopotamus is pink? Cool stuff like that. But my mom's boyfriend, Frank . . . He told me . . ."

My stomach tangled.

"He told me," she finally managed, "that I was 'socially unprepared for the real world.' That kids my age might think I'm weird. That maybe I *was* weird. And I . . . I was too embarrassed to tell my mom what Frank said. Because he's right, isn't he? A few months ago he even signed me up for Girl Scouts, so that I could 'socialize.' But I couldn't get over what he said. So I barely spoke at all. Then I quit." She drew in a tiny breath. "Anyway, promise you won't think that's weird, okay? Even after you get to know me?"

I didn't know how to answer her. I didn't think she expected me to. Still, I desperately wanted to do something. To help her. To *feel* with her. What might a real cat say, in this situation?

Calling on all my vocal chords, I gave a slight *murrr* followed by a low-pitched *aaaauuuuh*. It wasn't nearly enough. It didn't tell her that *life is so curious on Earth*; it didn't say, *You don't deserve this*. But hopefully it reminded her: *You are not alone.*

"Thanks, Leonard," Olive said, then flicked off the lamp.

I lay there feeling very much like I'd dodged one

thing—and stepped directly into something else. Weird? Olive? Weird meant *unearthly*, and Olive was firmly of this Earth. As an outsider, even I could identify her as human: someone who lived and belonged and spoke with intention. So I guess you could say the idea startled me, that Frank might not see what I saw, not feel what I felt. Olive had rescued me in a storm. She'd given me a place to stay, these blankets beneath my paws. How could anyone see her as anything but good? As anything but purely, wonderfully human?

I flitted, turned. And I thought about Olive—whom I trusted. Whom I trusted from the second we met. If she could share something so personal with me, then why couldn't I share more with her?

That might put your species at risk, a voice in me said.

Olive is not just any human, another part of me argued. Wouldn't it be so much easier, if I could just tell her what I was?

Very carefully, I started weighing my choices. If I snuck into a car, could I guarantee that it was traveling in the right direction? If I tried to board an airplane by myself, wouldn't someone notice me? On my journey, what would happen if a human discovered that I had no earthly home? What if they thought I might be "better off" in a shelter, trapped in a wire cage, with no method of escape? But Olive—Olive had human hands and a mouth that could speak words like *may we borrow this car to drive cross-country?* Or *one airplane ticket, please, to travel with my cat.*

Rolling on the bed, I let the idea wash over me.

Was telling Olive my only chance of returning home?

14

That Tuesday, Norma's truck still wasn't working, so Q picked us up on his way to the aquarium, rolling down the windows as he approached. "Leonard, my man!"

I stared at him, sticking my head between the porch rails, and thought, *Is there a good way to tell a human: I am not like you?* Would revealing my secret put the hive at risk, if I only told *one* trustworthy person?

"Got you something," Q said, climbing the stairs with a bundle in his hands. "Now, it isn't much, and I'm not expecting a thank-you card, but . . ."

On the porch, he bent to my level and showed me what he'd brought: a collar. My own collar. And a harness and a leash.

"I get it," he said. "You're not a dog, so you're probably thinking, 'What the heck is this for?' But if you're going to hang around with us, we've got to take some precautions. This way, you can be out and about."

The collar was sleek and black, with a silver tag that said LEONARD. He slipped the loop over my head, and there it rested—snug but comfortably—on my neck.

"You hate it?" Q asked.

Quite the opposite. It hadn't occurred to me that cats could wear collars, that I'd be allowed this bit of clothing. It wasn't a ranger's uniform. It wasn't a Hawaiian shirt. But it was shiny, reflective, and could help keep me safe.

Just like that, I was purring.

At first it alarmed me, the way my body was vibrating. I briefly wondered if this was the beginning of another panic attack, if a second trip to the vet was in store. But the feeling wasn't unpleasant. Actually, it was great—like I was untouchable and warm and pleased from the inside out.

"Good cat," Q said, chuckling. "Very good."

A minute later, Norma appeared on the porch, examining me. "Shouldn't we have him stay here, let him get some rest?"

I countered that with a series of wails, practically flinging myself downstairs.

"Leonard has spoken," Q said, loading me into

the car as the sky turned purple. It was one of those dusky summer afternoons, when the temperature hovered high, and it *almost* rained—but then the clouds pulled back, and there it was: a brilliantly clear evening.

"Once a week, we come in at night to clean up," Q explained. "It's so packed now during the day. Can't even elbow your way through the crowd, much less clean."

Chilled air whooshed past us as Norma, Olive, Q, and I slipped into the aquarium. Humans, especially those who live by the beach, turn up the air-conditioning until their skin prickles, throwing on sweatshirts to regulate their body temperatures. Since it was past closing time, with the halls empty except for staff, Norma grabbed Olive a sweatshirt from the gift shop, slapping a stack of money by the register. Olive said thank you, pulling the hoodie over her overalls.

"Well," Q said, clapping his hands. "Time to get to it."

We passed signs for creatures of the deep, with names much more alien than mine: BIGNOSE UNICORNFISH, BIG-BELLIED SEAHORSE, AFRICAN PANCAKE TORTOISE, CLOWNFISH, FOXFACE RABBITFISH, GIANT PACIFIC OCTOPUS. Norma pointed out a few exhibits to Olive, who nodded in concentration. Listening to them speak, I made connections: that Olive's dad was Norma's son; that Q had worked here the longest; that—after the shrimping industry dried up in South Carolina—Norma switched from captain of a boat to captain of the aquarium. She provided daily care, rehabilitation, and record keeping for all the marine animals.

Mostly I just watched, relaxing a little. I watched them clean the exhibits. I watched them scrape the scum from rocks and skim the water with nets. They threw slivers of sardines into the sparkling tanks and traced their fingers along the glass, smiling as the sea lions followed. They switched on music called "The Beach Boys" and mopped the floors to a swishing beat. A small part of me despised the dampness under my paws, but other than that, everything felt . . . close to calm.

"I am the poet of the Body," a famous human once said. "I am the poet of the Soul." And I wondered if that's what I was seeing in them, in these people. Body and soul.

"Okay," Q said after a while. "This calls for ice cream. I don't know what 'this' is, but ice cream is almost always called for."

Norma said, "You two go on. I've got a date with a scrubber brush."

In the cafeteria, I seated myself on one of the chairs, my paws perched safely on the table—I'm not sure why this was funny, but apparently it was—and Q grabbed two small cups of vanilla ice cream.

"So," he said, handing Olive a plastic spoon. "Your grandma says that you might be moving to California soon, starting a new school."

Olive winced and dug into the ice cream. "Yeah. I don't know. That's Frank's idea."

"You don't want to go? I understand that. But they've got some awesome animals in California: golden trout, coyotes, California crocodile . . ."

"I love crocodiles," Olive said. "And alligators. Did you know that they can weigh over one thousand pounds? And you wouldn't think it, but their muscles aren't really that strong when they open their mouths. Like, if you wanted to, you could hold their jaws shut, with nothing but your hands. And their eggs are . . ." Olive paused, setting down her spoon. "Sorry."

Q frowned. "Sorry for what?"

"I'm being weird, with all the animal facts. That's what some people say."

"Some people who?"

Olive shrugged.

"Let me ask you a question," Q said after a moment, leaning back in his chair. "Do you think *I'm* weird?" Just then, he screwed up his face, puffing out his cheeks, widening his eyeballs like a fish.

Olive tried, very unsuccessfully, to suppress a grin.

"That's what I thought. Now, I don't want to feed you some junk like 'everyone's on their own path,' but in a way it's true. There are people who take the roads and people who take the marshlands. You, my friend, don't seem like a road taker. Anytime you want to talk about animals, I'm all ears." Q took a breath, reaching over to pat the crest of my head. "But hey, you've got the summer to figure everything out. Figure out exactly who you want to be."

Something told me that maybe he was talking to me, too.

That night, after returning from the aquarium, Olive asked to keep me. Keep me, for real.

I was listening next to the refrigerator, Stanley panting by my side.

"I'll walk him and everything," Olive was saying on the phone. "Yes, Mom, walk him. He's good on a leash. Mmm-hmm. I know. I *know*. But you haven't even seen him! He's really cute and well behaved, and he hasn't scratched me or bitten me or anything. And he even uses the litter box—most of the time! It's a big responsibility. I get it. But I'm also thinking . . . if we move to California with Frank . . ."

Olive paused. She sucked in a breath.

"Is it so bad," she said, "to want a friend?"

I couldn't let this go on any longer—not as Olive stood there in the kitchen, asking her mother: *Can I keep him?* Everything was stacking up: my will to live, my homesickness. And now I didn't want to disappoint Olive, this human girl who kept rescuing me over and over again. She was becoming attached. Wouldn't it be kinder to say something now?

"You hear that, Leonard?" Olive said, hanging up the phone. Excitement danced in her voice. "My mom said she'll consider it, which is a good sign. She wouldn't let me even *think* about a hamster. Or a rabbit."

She knelt down, stroking the underside of my chin. As she blinked at me, I knew that I had to be brave—like the fiercest of house cats—and tell her exactly what I was. How would she react? How horribly might this go? Anxiety surged in my stomach, but still, I mapped out a plan: *Tonight, find a crayon.*

You see, my methods for telling Olive were limited. Pencils were too sharp—a danger to the eyes. Pens could burst, staining the white patches of my fur. Crayons were absolutely the answer: beautifully colored wax sticks that were also incredibly safe. Human children used them, so how difficult could they be?

We went to bed. After Olive flicked off the lamp, her turtle night-light glowing, I scoured the house: at the bottom of backpacks, in the ceramic kitchen bowls, under tables and chairs. Luckily, there was a big box of crayons in the downstairs closet—ninety-six colors, sorted into shades. As a cat, my eyes were most sensitive to blues, greens, and yellows. I'm not sure if this is true for all felines, or perhaps just me, but I could see *some* browns, some orange tones. Still, I had a hard time choosing between SEPIA and RAW SIENNA, but eventually I selected the second: it was more E.T.'s shade of brown.

I set to work the next morning as the humans ate breakfast; I figured it was better to work undisturbed. Rather quickly, it became apparent that gripping the crayon with my front paws was a disastrous plan. I couldn't write straight enough. My mouth—my mouth was the key. Crunching the crayon with my back molars, I could just about steady it. True, my tongue was watering from the bitterness, and I had to breathe vigorously through my nose to keep from choking, but once I got the hang of it, I was surprised by how cleanly the crayon wrote. It was a warm day, and the wax drifted onto the walls.

Spitting out the crayon with an exaggerated hack, I stepped back to admire my work. The word ALIEN was haphazardly scrawled in brown letters, over a foot high, just above Olive's baseboard. I'll admit that panic did seize me. I was really doing this. Olive would see my work; she would know. Part of me asked, *What if she is afraid of you?* Another part said, *What if she tells the world?* I sat stiffly by the words, taller than me, and bid my time—preparing for the inevitable shock of Olive's reaction.

The fur tingled between the pads of my toes.

I began mildly hyperventilating.

And Olive breezed in fifteen minutes later, asking if I'd seen her copy of *Wild Animals and Beyond*—a book she was reading and enjoying, too. "It was right here," she said, lifting up her pillow. "I swore that's where I left it."

I cleared my throat, flicked my tail toward ALIEN, and braced myself. This was it.

"Oh!" she said, vision skating right past me. "In the kitchen. I think I left it in the kitchen. You coming, Leonard?"

Alien! I shouted after her. *I am an alien!*

But she was already halfway down the stairs, then she was sliding on a pair of yellow sandals, grabbing a beach towel and her book. I followed, caterwauling as she began heading in the direction of the ocean, as the screen door slapped behind us. My tail fuzzed, whiskers pulling back. Everything was happening so fast—so *wrongly*—that it floored me. Here I was, shouting after a human, desperately trying to tell her that I was not of this world, and the human was grabbing my harness.

"I haven't gone to the beach at all this summer," Olive said, holding my gaze at the bottom of the steps. Gently, she slipped the harness over my head, clicked the buckle, and attached a leash. "I'm not really a beach person, but it just seems kind of silly to be so close to the water and not go. You sure you'd like to come?"

I didn't know how to convey it: that I wanted her to rush back upstairs and read my message. What if someone else found it first? There was always the possibility that other members of my species were correct about humans. That if humans discovered us, our lives would change for the worse.

I *was* curious about the beach, though—despite the danger of the ocean. You could just glimpse the sea from the porch, a wavy line of pure blue. On Earth, everything is water this, water that. Have you drunk enough water? Have you released enough water? Did you clean yourself with water this morning?

"Watch out for cars," Olive said. "And for Norma. This is definitely not on the schedule, but she's working on her motorcycle today—and I didn't want to bother her by asking."

None of this reassured me.

The concrete was warm beneath my paws, a harsh breeze ruffling my bib. We ambled along a sidewalk edged by palm trees, other humans passing us in small motorized vehicles—golf carts, someone called them. *Danger mobiles*, I renamed them; they made a dull whirring noise as they zipped by ice cream shops, restaurants, and a store that advertised "boogie boards." I couldn't imagine what those were, but they sounded so festive, so delightfully human.

The sun was yellowish as we reached the shore,

and my eyes were everywhere at once: on a wooden pier with spindly legs, casting itself out to sea; on the millions and millions of specks of sand; on the humans playing ball sports, laughing and sunning themselves by the water. A part of me expected to join them. We'd brought a beach towel, hadn't we? From what I'd detected, we were supposed to splay ourselves atop this towel, and rotate our bodies as the sun hit. But that was not what we did. We stayed back. We observed.

The truth is, we hid.

At the base of a sand dune, Olive wrapped my leash around her wrist, and then tucked herself in front of the tall grasses, her knees to her chest. She was wearing her faded-blue overalls and a pair of tinted sunglasses; I could see my reflection in the lenses, staring up at her with a question: *This is what we do?*

"Maybe I'll just read," Olive said, opening her book to the middle. She didn't read, though. And she didn't talk to me much after that. It wasn't an uncomfortable silence—not exactly. But over the last couple of days I'd gotten used to her voice. She'd told me interesting facts: *Did you know that three percent of Antarctic ice is penguin urine?* She'd told me she wanted to be a veterinarian. Or a zookeeper. Or a wildlife biologist. She'd told me things confidently, like I understood. Now her body language was changing—back hunching, bare feet digging into the sand.

And it kept coming in flashes: what I'd written on Olive's bedroom wall.

Soon, she'd know.

I batted a few blades of grass with my paws, examining the beach. Families—so many families here: parents passing out bags of food, children slapping the water in their inflatable wings. I couldn't look at them for long. It's difficult to see something and think, *That will never be me.* Our species isn't born; we're *created*: a collision of particles, a rearrangement of matter. No parents. No siblings.

I snapped my attention elsewhere. Not far away, a pod of young humans was thwacking a firm white ball over a net—back and forth, back and forth. Every once in a while, they peered in our direction, covering their mouths with their hands. They were laughing. The noise rattled in an unpleasant way, crawling into the depth of my belly.

On this planet, every noise is two noises. Sometimes laughter is like Olive and Q, joking at the aquarium about stick horses and sharks named Steve and

Martin; and sometimes laughter is like the spike of a stingray or the teeth of a leopard seal.

Olive tensed.

And I felt like panting. The weather was becoming unbearably hot, and I was counting down to our moment of return, when Olive would see the word *ALIEN*. Did cats pant? Maybe that was dogs, or—

"Is she going to stop *staring*?" one of young humans snapped, just loud enough for us to hear. Like the rest of his clan, he was dressed in slick fabric, presumably used for bathing. "Did she . . . did she bring her *cat* to the beach?"

I didn't have much time to react. Olive just bolted, barely stopping to brush the sand off her overalls. Were overalls traditional beach attire? Human clothing was, for the most part, a mystery to me; I knew what I liked: Hawaiian shirts, vests with plenty of useful pockets. But I found it strange—the idea that there is a "right" kind of clothing. So you want to visit the beach in overalls? Or a turtleneck? Or a pair of green trousers with a matching scarf? What does it matter? How could it possibly impact anyone else?

At the end of the boardwalk, Olive scooped me up. We were weaving through a crowd, through a sea of golf carts and frozen-lemonade stands. She was breathing rather heavily, an unnatural wheeze like I'd experienced right before the vet. There was water running down her face.

No, *tears*—real human tears.

And I had no idea how to help her.

People have a terrible reputation in our galaxy. War, pollution, the treatment of whales—all of these are distinctly human. But there are also the smaller offenses: their drinking straws, their boxes within boxes. Why ship boxes inside further boxes, only to throw the outer box away? It is terribly wasteful.

My point is, there was already a strong case against humans. That they suffered from greed and gluttony; that they were impulsive and easy to anger, while we were logical always. But I'd seen *I Love Lucy*. I'd seen pictures of human families, with their communal meals and their board games, and I knew—I just *knew*—there was more to them.

Yet as we fled the beach, I wondered: Was I so entranced with their dinner forks and their television sets that I'd missed something? Had I misjudged them as a species?

Back at the house, Olive slid me onto the kitchen countertop and poured herself a glass of orange juice, glugging it down. "I was at the beach with my cat," she finally said, as if this clarified everything. "My *cat.* How can I fix being weird if I'm doing something weird and I don't even know it?"

Anxiously, I trailed her to the bedroom, where she pulled out a small computer from a dresser drawer. Patting the bed, she settled back into the pillows, and I sprang up beside her, pawing at her stomach: *Look! Look at the wall! I am an alien.*

"Sometimes I wish I were a cat," Olive said, opening her laptop. "I think I'd make a much better cat than a person."

Suddenly there was an empty bar on the computer screen, and she typed inside it: *How to be normal.* The words appeared in a miraculous, blinking flash. (This! This was so much easier than a crayon.) Other searches followed. *How to make new friends. First day in California school. Signs you are hopelessly weird.* And every result sunk her a little lower. It was hard to watch. By the fifth search, I'd almost stopped trying to direct her attention to the wall and started thinking about ways to tell her: *You are a perfectly acceptable version of a human, exactly as you are.*

Eventually she sniffled and said, "Ah, I need a tissue. Be right back."

She left me alone with the laptop.

She left me alone with an opportunity.

I figured that I didn't have much time—maybe a minute or less—so I made the most of it, selecting the appropriate keys with swift punches of my paws, my ears pulled back in panicked concentration. Human fingers would've been incredibly helpful, and much more accurate. Several times, I pressed too long, on three keys instead of one; the message turned from **hello olive** to **hello olivehhhhhjjjjhhhhnnn**, which just wouldn't do. I erased. I typed faster, fear and courage welling up inside me.

"Leonard, what are you . . ." Olive said, returning from the bathroom. There was a tissue bunched in the palm of her hand. "Are you trying to write on my keyboard?"

Exactly! I thought at first, before realizing she was joking. I was a cat to her. Only a cat. Cats did not type perfectly intelligible messages inside Internet search bars. And yet—

Olive rounded the corner of the bed, gazing down at the screen.

And she saw.

She stood there, unmoving, for so long, perhaps reading the words over and over, trying to draw meaning from them. hello olive, I'd typed. it is me leonard i am an alien do not be scared. Could I have phrased it better? Who knows. I did my best. And I just hoped that Olive would understand.

Her head snapped to look at me then, her eyes wide, pupils enlarging. I could tell that her mouth was dry, because she swallowed three times in a row: big, gasping gulps. Physically, I wasn't sure how to react. A small part of me was relieved for the secret to be out in the open. A far greater part was waiting for Olive to say something. Anything. For her to scream, shout, acknowledge me. Should I extend a paw, offer to shake her hand, now that we were being properly introduced? *No, no, don't be silly.* Besides, I was too anxious to move.

"This isn't happening," Olive finally said, as if trying to convince herself. "There's . . . there's no way." Her voice was quivering, like a thin ripple on water.

My assumption was that I should stay incredibly still—no sudden movements. Sudden movements might frighten her away. Slowly, I lowered myself onto my belly, paws folded beneath me, but then I realized: it looked like I was about to pounce. I abandoned the whole position.

"This is *not* possible," Olive said more firmly, but I could see the doubt sweeping in. Hadn't she said it herself, that I was an exceptional cat? For a long moment, we held each other's gaze; and then, eventually, she reached over—hand quaking—and deleted my words.

"I don't . . . I don't know how this can be real," she said, sliding the laptop toward me. "But if it *is* real, if this is really happening, I'm going to need you to do that again. Please?"

Would Olive have preferred a normal cat? Or was the possibility of something more—something like me—intriguing to her? Either way, I typed. I turned letters into words, my throat constricting from the stress of it all. I didn't want to say the same thing over again—what purpose would that serve? Instead, I wrote: i am from another planet and need your help getting home, adding a *please* at the last moment, just as Olive had.

She kept taking in deep breaths, only to push them dramatically out. She read the screen three or four times, looked at me—and then promptly fled the room, slamming the door behind her. Not the ideal reaction. I couldn't help but feel a little hurt.

On the other side of the wall, I could hear her pacing back and forth, mumbling to herself. String after string of words, all running together: "You're not this weird, you're imagining things, pull yourself together, come on, think, stop and just think."

My ears pointed back nervously, because I didn't expect this. She wasn't scared of me; she was scared of *herself*. And I wanted to tell her that everything would be okay, if we could just talk this through. But I couldn't open the door. I didn't know how to dangle with that kind of precision. So I settled for a frenzied kneading of the blankets, my paws massaging the soft fabric. Oddly, this calmed some of my nerves.

Until I heard her bolting down the stairs.

Which panicked me again. Here I was, trapped inside the room. With water, yes. With food, yes. But time was moving very slowly. Time can do that on Earth. When Olive didn't come back around lunchtime, I gave up kneading the blankets and jumped onto the windowsill, tucking myself behind the curtains. I could see the whole neighborhood from there: rows of greenery and houses on stilts, hydrangea bushes and golf carts. And Olive. Olive striding back and forth, hands gripping the sides of her hair, looking very much like she was about to fall apart.

I felt terrible. Maybe that's too simple a statement to encompass everything that was building inside me, but I'm not sure I can explain it any other way: an aching, hollow sensation that grows and grows. But why was I feeling *so* terrible? I began purring just to calm myself, and sat there, vibrating on the windowsill, my lungs fluttering wildly.

It was almost three hours before Olive returned, opening the door, peeking inside. I'm not sure what she was expecting to see—if she thought she'd imagined me entirely. But there I was, paws-deep in blankets again.

"Okay," she said, still breathing in little gasps. "Please tell me this is real, because right now I'm thinking that I am *by far* the weirdest kid on the planet. I need confirmation that you are who you say you are, and it's not just me." Cautiously, she switched on the laptop again and gestured for me to type—if I wanted to, if I could. So I hunted and pecked at the letters, trying to get the message exactly right.

you are not weird you are of this earth, I responded. **what confirmation do you need.**

"I don't know," she said shakily. "I think it's the computer. It needs to be more than the computer. What if someone's playing a prank on me or something? I don't know how they could get into my laptop, but maybe they did."

Quickly, I typed, **look wall behind you**, and she turned to see the scratching of a brown crayon, written thinly on the paint.

"How did I *miss* that?" she said. "Alien. Okay. You're an alien . . . I'm going to sit down." Her knees buckled as she leaned back on the bed. There was a slight tremor in her hands. Earlier that week, I'd seen Stanley lick Olive's fingers—a long slurp with his enormous tongue—but something told me that cats didn't lick humans with the same frequency. My tongue felt like sandpaper, even to me. So I let my animal instincts guide me, moving onto Olive's lap and headbutting her gently in the face.

And I kept it there, my skull to her nose. Here's what I was hoping to communicate: that I meant no harm, and that this wasn't just in her head.

"Your fur is going up my nose," she said.

I pulled back.

"I'm still not sure if any of this is real. Can you give me some time?"

I nodded.

"Did you just nod?"

I nodded again.

And she told me, in a quiet way, "This is all very astonishing."

We stayed up incredibly late that night, talking and typing. At some point, Stanley scooted his way to the foot of the bed, splaying himself on the blue rug. And we built a tent around him, Olive grabbing a sheet from the linen closet and draping it across some chairs. In the light of the miniature turtle, the lint from the fabric looked like stars.

"Tell me about it," she said, still wary, but warming to me. "What's it like, where you're from?"

beautiful, I wrote. **safe. i am never alone.**

My forelegs were becoming sore from all the typing, all the careful pressing of letters, but I was aching to write. It felt like someone, for the first time, was really listening.

Olive rested her chin in her hands, leaning cautiously closer. "What else? Tell me more."

my planet is made of helium.

"Helium?" she asked. "I thought helium was just a gas, like for balloons and stuff."

humans have much to learn.

"I bet we do. I bet we don't even know half of what's out there. I mean, people are still debating who built Stonehenge."

the venusians.

Olive batted her eyes. "What?"

that is who built stonehenge.

"Oh," Olive said, clearly stunned. "Wow. I'm guessing those are aliens? The *ven-ooo-sians*." She pronounced it perfectly. "What's your species called, then? I don't even know the name of your planet."

it does not translate well.

"Just try."

need paper and crayon.

"That's a funny name for a planet."

no I need them.

"Oh, sorry! Sorry. It's been a long day."

She handed me a piece of paper along with raw sienna, which had rolled next to her nightstand. Carefully, with the crayon gripped in my mouth, I drew a spherical symbol, adding the strings—like ribbons fluttering around a balloon.

"That's the name?" Olive held the paper up to the turtle light. "It's cool. If you squint, it kind of reminds me of a moon jellyfish."

what is moon jellyfish, I asked, and she told me in a rather animated way. She told me lots of things: not just what a moon jellyfish was, but also that her daisy barrettes were a gift from her father, when she was still very small; that Frank was charming with everyone else, just not with her; and that she'd do just about anything to have a conversation with a penguin. "Their *flippers*," she said. "The way they *waddle*." And every once in a while, I'd catch her peering at me intently, when she thought I wasn't looking—studying me, as I'd studied her.

"How old are you?" she asked.

300, I typed.

"Wow," she said. "That's really old. Oh, I mean, no offense! I wish . . . I wish that everyone could live that long."

i am not offended, I said—then wondered, as Olive's eyes misted at the corners, if she was thinking of her dad.

"So are you . . . what's the word?"

immortal.

"Yes, that."

not on this planet.

Olive frowned. "Why would you risk it, then? Earth is dangerous." Before I could respond, she added, "Are you always a cat? Like, are there just a bunch of cats, floating in space? Sorry, too many questions. It's just all so much . . . But how does it *work*? I want to know everything."

I stretched my paws, flexing my toes. What I was about to write would require concentration, stamina, and punctuation. I still hadn't figured out capital letters on the keyboard, but commas and periods, those were fine. My chest fluttered, because it was rather scary—getting the words right, putting your fate in someone else's hands. As I clacked away, Olive read over my shoulder.

i wanted to be human and was supposed to be, I typed. but there was a mistake, i miscalculated the formula. my species is pure energy. we live as one, much like the drops in your ocean. humans should not know about us, but i believe in the goodness of most people, the goodness in you, and i am stuck here, i miss home and i do not want to die, so i need your help getting to yellowstone national park by july 21 at 9:01 a.m., coordinates 44.4605 degrees north, 110.8281 degrees west. please. please.

I typed *please* twice for extra politeness.

Digesting my message, Olive puffed out her cheeks with air, and then squashed her face with her palms.

I added, i hope this is not asking for too much. please.

"I'll help you, Leonard," Olive said uneasily. "Of course I'll help. It's just that I still have so many questions, and—" She snapped her gaze to me, dark hair whipping. "Wait, should I still call you Leonard? Do you have another name?"

leonard is nice, I told her honestly.

"Good," she said. "So, we have to go to Yellowstone specifically?"

yellowstone is my pickup point. my entire species must collect me. they have other stops along the way, to collect other travelers on other planets. they will know to find me at yellowstone, nowhere else.

Olive bit her lip. "The thing is, I'm only eleven, so I don't really have a car . . . or know how to drive, or even really know how to ride the bus across the country, so . . . I'll have to think of something. But I will think of something, okay?"

She didn't sound too convinced.

Strangely, I still had faith in her.

We pulled more blankets into the fort, the three of

us huddled together. Stanley let out a gigantic snore, and I curled into a loose ball, resting my muscles. It was actually rather nice, falling asleep in a tent. As a ranger, I would've spent a great deal of time beneath a canvas sky at night, and in the daytime identifying wildflowers, cooking stew.

"Hey, Leonard?" Olive said, very awake, just as I was drifting off. "You don't have to worry. I'll keep your secret . . . And I wanted you to know, I think it's sad that you didn't get to be human. You would've made a really nice one."

Silently, I told her thank you.

"I'm not sure how to ask this," she said. "Are there, like, any human things I can get for you? Anything you really want? Just think about it."

I didn't have to think about it. I already knew. Gathering the last bit of my strength for the night, I waddled to the keyboard.

And I typed: **raincoat**.

18

It had a hood and little black buttons. The yellow material was stiff—stiffer than I thought it'd be—but once Olive slipped it over my forelegs, down across my back, I found that I could move quite nicely. Gazing at myself in the bathroom mirror, it occurred to me that I looked somewhat like Olive in the flood. Our raincoats matched, almost exactly.

"I hope it's what you had in mind," Olive said as I twirled on the sink basin, examining myself from all angles. It fit snugly around me, stopping right before my tail. "I got it from Mrs. Kowalski down the street. She has this tiny dog who doesn't use it anymore."

Would I have preferred an umbrella? Would I have liked to clasp my human fingers around the handle and skip in rubber boots through the rain? Of course. But this was the next best thing—and I must say that it meant a lot, for Olive to deliver it so quickly. It was barely ten o'clock, the morning after our talk, and plans were already in motion.

"So here's the way I see it," Olive said as I jumped down from the sink. She was perched on the edge of the tub, bare feet tapping the tile floor. "I've been up all night thinking about how to get you to Yellowstone, and I realized that I can't do it by myself—not without driving a car and breaking the law. I'm going to have to ask Norma for help, which means coming up with a good excuse to go."

I nodded, ears forward. This seemed reasonable.

"But there's a catch," Olive said, grimacing. "She has this *huge* event on July eighteenth. It's a Save the Sea Turtles thing, and it's a really big deal for her job. Turtle Beach puts on a humongous festival for a week ahead of time; the whole town comes together. Norma has a bunch of planning to do ahead of time. And I know she won't miss it, no matter what I tell her, so . . . Could you wait that long?"

Could I? Theoretically, yes. If we left the evening of the eighteenth, that gave us two full days of travel, plus the nights—plenty of time. But waiting until nearly the end of July was risky. What if Norma said she'd take us, and then changed her mind? What if something happened to me in the meantime?

"Waiting could be dangerous," Olive said, like she was reading my thoughts. "But based on Google maps, it's only thirty-four hours in a car, and I honestly can't think of another way. Even if I got you to Yellowstone much earlier, what would I do? I couldn't stay with you for the month, and I couldn't *leave* you there—not with all the wild animals. Bears and house cats aren't usually friends." She twisted her lips. "I *could* tell Norma you're an alien, and that we need to get you home sooner . . . but we've never had a conversation about anything serious. I wouldn't even know where to begin. What if she thinks I'm making it all up? Or that I've lost it? What if she sends me back to my mom, because she doesn't want to talk it through? And if *that* happens, what would happen to you? I couldn't live with myself if—"

Just then, there was a knock at the bathroom door, and the rasp of Norma's voice behind it: "Olive? You on the phone?"

Olive bolted up from the tub. "Um, yes! Yes, I am! I'm talking on the phone."

Norma paused on the other side of the door. "Is it your mom?"

"Yep! My mom!"

"All right, then. Tell her I said hello."

"I will!" Olive said, much louder than necessary.

"Remember we're leaving for the aquarium in a minute."

"Yep!"

The two of us listened for Norma's footsteps, clomping on the hardwood, back into the kitchen. Olive released a gusty breath. "That was too close. Norma's one thing, but in public, if someone catches us talking, it could turn out *really* bad. Do you remember *E.T.*? I don't want the government to come and take you away, or study you, or . . . worse."

Worse? Immediately, I thought of every warning I'd ever received. *Never trust a human.*

"The raincoat's fine," Olive said, "but we can't talk like this outside of the house, okay?" She leaned in, adjusting the stiff fabric. "Here, you missed a button."

I wore my raincoat to the aquarium, partly because I looked quite snazzy in it. It also added a shield to my fur, protecting me from danger.

"Leonard, my friend," Q said, greeting us in the lobby. "Wowee, that is some outfit."

"He's normal!" Olive practically shouted, then lowered her voice. "I mean, lots of cats wear outfits."

"'Course," Q said, like this was normal indeed. "Now, who wants to feed some stingrays?"

All around us were tourists, cameras swinging from their necks. I noticed that quite a few of them were looking at me—a cat in a raincoat, on a leash, in an aquarium. I considered that maybe I should be making a better effort to blend in. Would these people really try to hurt me if they understood what I was? If they knew about my home planet? Just in case, I curled up, lifting one of my hind legs straight into the air, and proceeded to groom myself—licking my fur in swift strokes, nibbling at the soft underside of my belly. This was quite difficult to do in a raincoat, but I still managed, like a real cat would.

Olive gently pulled at my leash, and together we wove through the growing crowd. Q led us into the shark tunnel, where we paused to find Steve and Martin, circling rhythmically above us. "I've worked here every day for twenty years," Q said, "and these guys *still* amaze me."

Out of curiosity I rose onto my hind legs, pressing my front paws against the tank, avoiding a nose bump this time. The glass extended all the way to the floor, so I had a clear view of everything—fine-grained sand, mountains of coral, fish darting in schools. They were speaking to one another, too: changing their shape as a group, communicating with body language and sound. Through the glass, I could hear them croaking, purring, popping.

The whole school noticed me then, a hundred sets of eyes gazing in my direction. I flexed my back, standing taller. Maybe they'd never seen a cat. Or maybe they identified something different about me, something not quite ordinary. Because gradually they swam over, until they were inches from the glass. I was vaguely aware of the humans around me, turning to one another and whispering, but mostly I was trying not to be rude. Earlier in the week, I'd witnessed Q speaking to the fish; I figured that I should do the same.

You, they were asking. *You, you, you?*

Hardly the most intelligent conversation, but I responded in kind: purring through the glass, bobbing my head. *Yes*, I said. *Yes, yes, yes.*

Here? they said. *Here, here?*

Yes! I said. *Yes, yes.*

This continued for, oh, I don't know. Two minutes? Three? Not long in the scope of things, but soon there was a gentle tap on my back. Olive bent down to my level.

"People are staring," she said nervously, picking me

up and striding away, my neck craned over her shoulder. Someone flashed a camera. Someone waved. I told myself that a cat shouldn't wave back.

"I'm serious, Leonard," Olive said in the staff room. "We have to be *much* more careful. People can never find out about you." She plopped us down, eyes wide. It took her a long while to say her next words, but when she did, they ran together, fast and blurted. "Can-you-talk-to-*fish*?"

Startled, my whiskers twitched. Was it really so extraordinary? Hadn't Q spoken with them, too? I nodded, then readjusted my raincoat, which had slipped to the side.

"Every time I think that things can't get any stranger . . ." Olive said, leaning against the wall.

Q knocked on the staff room door, strutting in. "Leonard, my man, you're about to cause a riot. They love you out there." He paused, thinking. "We need to get this cat a T-shirt. Make him a real employee. Leonard, I'm telling you, you're going places."

So we went to the gift shop, where Olive selected an extremely small size, fit for a human toddler. On it was a stingray, coasting through blue waters, which was very appealing, indeed.

It was hours before we could speak privately, back at the beach house. Norma was lighting citronella torches on the porch, swatting away the mosquitoes; my ears were picking up the sound of marsh grass dancing gently in the summer breeze; and Olive kept checking over her shoulder. When we were in the kitchen—alone except for Stanley—she brought out the computer and set it on the table. The keys lit up.

"Do you think you can speak to all animals?" Olive asked quietly. "Like Doctor Dolittle?"

I hopped onto the table and quietly pressed the keys. **q talked to fish. who is do little.**

"Oh," Olive said. "Q was pretending. And Doctor Dolittle is in a movie. He can talk to animals like you. It's just, it's amazing. More than amazing. Have you talked to Stanley?"

At the sound of his name, Stanley began panting contentedly, the side of his tongue drifting from his mouth. His lips were black on the outside and pink underneath. *The birds*, he told me again, eyes flickering.

stanley says much, I typed.

Olive perched on the edge of a chair. "What does he—"

"Got Chinese," Norma said, thumping into the

kitchen, takeout bags in hand. She stopped short by the fridge, eyebrow raising at the computer—then at us. "What's all this?"

"Nothing," Olive said quickly, slamming the laptop shut.

"Because it looked like—"

"Mmm, eggrolls. Do you want to watch some TV? I think there's a new movie on Channel Seven, and we should . . . Yeah, let's watch that."

It took a long time for my heart rate to settle back down. They began viewing a program about whales, and I curled into the corner of the couch, wondering how long it would take for Olive to tell Norma about Yellowstone. How would she say the words?

"So, how's it working with Q?" Norma asked. "He's a good buddy of mine, but you can . . ." She cleared her throat. "You can always tag along with me and the sea lions."

"Thanks," Olive said, biting into an eggroll. I could tell she was distracted. She chewed and chewed. "Um, are you going anywhere this summer?"

Norma frowned, resting her fork by the rice. "Come again?"

"Like . . . are you going on any trips?"

"Don't plan to," she said, shaking her head. "But my

truck's out of the shop—and my sidecar's almost fixed up, too, if you want to hitch a ride somewhere local. Hilton Head? Kiawah Island? We could . . . visit some of my old fishing spots, maybe? Only local, though—I think we've got a good thing going on here. Wouldn't want to mess up the routine."

Olive opened her mouth several times to respond, but she didn't. Maybe she couldn't. It hit me then, in a way that I was unprepared for: the burden I'd placed on her. How much I was asking.

And how little I was giving in return.

19

I had wanted to become a ranger, in large part, to help humans. Back on my home planet, I'd seen an image broadcast to the hive by a previous visitor to Earth: a picture of an old, tattered photo ripped from a 1940s magazine. In it was a man with rugged brown shorts and a hat that shielded him from the sun. He was guiding a group of humans—somewhat heroically— through a wildflower meadow. Immediately, I could imagine myself in that role: Introducing people to the wonders of the natural world. Running my fingers over the tops of marigolds. Explaining pollination as the petals tickled my skin.

Had I lost sight of this? Stay undetected, stay alive—that was my focus since my arrival on Earth. I needed to travel home, back to my community and the infinite calmness of safety. But things were shifting. Shouldn't I do something for Olive in return?

I just couldn't think what.

Norma ate the rest of the eggrolls, then threw out the paper plates after Stanley vacuumed up the last bits of rice, lick by lick, with his enormous tongue. It was a brisk night, cooler than most, and the four of us lumbered to the beach, Olive dangling a flashlight in her hand. Moonlight pulsed over the sidewalk.

"You know about ghost crabs?" Norma said, searching the sand. "Got those funny little eyes."

"And they can change color to match their surroundings," Olive said, trudging up the boardwalk steps. "They eat sea turtle eggs, too."

"That's right. We had to protect the turtle nests much more than normal this year."

"When do they hatch? The turtles?"

"Soon," Norma said. "We just checked on them yesterday, and I'd say about a week. It'll be here before you know it."

Olive switched on her flashlight—the beam racing across the boardwalk—and suddenly I was chasing it, pouncing with excessive force, scrambling to catch the thin film of light. Did I think I would actually catch it? Perhaps part of me did. Stanley, on the other hand, was more interested in the seagulls that—every so often—dived into the grasses along-side us. I asked him to join in the yellow-light hunt (I would have felt less silly with company), but he just couldn't be bothered.

When we reached the beach, Olive slipped deeper and deeper into the dark. I followed her, of course—largely because we are friends, but also because, well, I was attached to a leash and had little choice in the matter. Norma and Stanley lagged behind as Olive and I tiptoed closer and closer to the waves. The sand was gritty underneath my paws, becoming wetter by the second, and I let out a solemn but pressing *meow*, asking Olive: *Can we stop here?*

Somehow she understood me, turning back to bend to my level. When we were eye to eye, I placed my paws on her knees and extended my face toward hers. "You know," she said very quietly, so only I could hear, "standing in the ocean is pretty human. You don't have to go in far at all, and I'll be right here, but you should experience it. I was thinking that I could give you human lessons, while I figure out how to tell Norma about Yellowstone."

Human lessons? The idea was intriguing. *Maybe she is right about the ocean*, I thought, my fur puffing slightly. Yet my mind brought me back to the flood—all alone in that tree—and I remembered just how much danger I was in that night. How Olive saved me then and would surely save me now, if the occasion called for it.

So I dropped my paws from her knees. My leash extended quite far, but Olive never strayed; she remained very much by my side as we stepped into the ocean. The first sweep hit my paws in a bubbly burst. *Cold.* It was colder than I expected for such a warm climate, but the feeling was not altogether terrible. In fact, it was refreshing.

Olive said, "It's pretty cool, isn't it?" And I flexed my toes, sand dimpling beneath me. With my night vision I could see the ocean's never-ending plane, extending on and on. Perhaps this is as close as humans will come to infinity: gazing out at the sea, toes in the water, feeling a part of something huge, yet being very, very small themselves.

I'm not sure how long we stood there. Eventually Stanley approached us, rolling his whole body in the shallow waters, then shaking out his great mane. He was at home here—in this town, in this ocean—and I wondered if I would ever have that much comfort anywhere. If I could give myself up entirely to a landscape and a moment and a feeling.

"It's getting late," Norma said after a while. "Should we head back?"

So we walked back, our reflections nothing but shadows on the ground—and that night I made a list at Olive's request, typing in the dim glow of the turtle night-light.

Human Lessons

1. Go to a real movie theater
2. The creation and enjoyment of poetry
3. Bowling and recreational board games
4. Preparation and consumption of a cheese sandwich
5. Host a dinner party

Sitting back on my haunches, looking at the list, I was rather impressed with the sophistication of the typing (I'd figured out capital letters with the help of the shift key); it was also dangerously brave, a list that would push me out of my comfort zone. Sure, I could have added more—a note about music or dancing or extreme sports. I could've written a never-ending list, because weren't there so many things? How could one possibly choose between the splendor of a midnight countdown, with party poppers (very tempting), and the humanness of baking a cake?

But we only had so much time.

Five things seemed good enough.

"A cheese sandwich?" Olive said, cross-legged in her striped pajamas. "I think we can give you a bite of one, but aren't cats lactose intolerant?"

I wasn't familiar with the word *lactose*, so I shrugged this off with a shiver of my fur.

Olive cocked her head. "The dinner party thing we can do. How many guests do you want, though? Because I don't really know anyone here, besides Norma and Q. It would have to be small."

Small is good, I typed at the bottom of the list. **Thank you thank you.**

"Welcome, welcome," Olive said, scratching just behind my ear. She was smiling in this peculiar way. "I still can't really believe this—any of it. I don't think that anything this extraordinary will ever happen to me again."

Probably not, I typed.

And for some reason, she laughed.

20

Please don't get me wrong. There were many terrible things about being a cat.

Pots and pans, the garbage disposal, the *whoosh* of the shower curtain—any loud noise sent me skittering; sometimes I bolted so quickly that it was difficult to slow down, the rug bunching beneath me. Houseplants were nice to shove in my mouth and chew, but my cat stomach couldn't take it. And I developed a worrying obsession with flinging myself at the window screens, clinging to them, climbing with my claws. Don't ask me why. I can't explain it myself.

But there were good things, too. My reflexes were sharp. Anything moving, darting, or flashing, I could see perfectly. And Olive—there was Olive. For a flicker of a second, as we spoke about my human lessons, a thought did occur to me: *Despite my homesickness, would it be the worst thing, to get stuck on Earth?*

I quickly swiped it away—and focused on the movies.

It may not surprise you to know that cats aren't allowed in movie theaters, that the seats are not formed to the size and shape of our bodies. There were so many places that I couldn't go, solely based on my fur, my claws, my relatively short legs. But *The Wizard of Oz* was playing at Turtle Beach Cinema for one night only, so Olive told me that we had to try.

"I just don't want to stick you in my backpack," she said as we were getting ready to go. "Not after what happened on the bus. Cats *really* shouldn't be in backpacks. But I'm trying to figure out the best way to sneak you in."

Norma was in the kitchen searching for her motor-cycle keys. I heard rustling, the smack of boots against the floor. "Got 'em," she finally said. "Ready?"

"Snap decision," Olive whispered to me. "I have an idea."

❀

"So," Norma said to Olive, "remind me again why you're wearing my windbreaker?"

We were standing in line at the movies. Well, I

wasn't standing. I was suspended in the bib of Olive's overalls, comfortably tucked underneath a large coat. She'd zipped it up to her neck, but there was plenty of air flow—thank goodness. The ride over in the motor-cycle's sidecar was rather touch and go; against every swerve, I tried not to grip too tightly. We'd made it, though, and surely that's what counted.

"It gets cold in the movies," Olive said, shifting from foot to foot.

"You look lumpy," Norma said.

Another human voice added, "Here you go! Two tickets to see *The Wizard*. Round the corner, to the left."

I felt Olive grab her ticket and scamper away, one hand clutching the coat zipper.

"Wait a second," Norma said behind us. "Olive. *Olive!*" It was the tone of Norma's voice: a deep, dawning realization. She knew I was under that jacket—and she wasn't pleased. Olive picked up the pace, moving rapidly through the hall. Or what I presumed was a hall: it was really very dark beneath the fabric. My heart thudded slightly with fear. Would Norma expose me—expose us—right here in the theater?

Abruptly Olive stopped, and I heard a door swinging open—then the sound of laughter and the smell of buttered popcorn, with all its salt and tang. The movies. No, I hadn't strolled in on my own two feet, but still: I was at the *movies*. An experience that would transform me, transport me—like it had for generations of humans. Who wouldn't want to see a chase on horses, a voyage on the sea, a flight to Earth's moon?

Olive settled in the back row; I know this because she unzipped the jacket, just a little, and I poked my head out, my eyes adjusting to the dimness. Before us was a massive blue screen and a theater dotted with people.

"Sailor," Norma whispered, scooting into our row. She looked frazzled, as if she'd been fighting with seagulls. "At first I thought, nope, no, you wouldn't do that. But by golly, you've really gone for it. And you brought him in the *motorcycle*?"

Norma and I locked eyes. It was difficult to tell if she was angry with me or impressed that I'd stayed undetected for so long.

"Up," she said. "Let's go."

"But we just got here," Olive said, guilt in her voice—for my discovery or for bringing me to the movies in the first place, I didn't know. "Can we stay, even just for a little bit?"

"Heck no," Norma said.

Disappointment filtered through me, my ears

pinning back. I was looking forward to this movie in particular, after Olive had discussed it with me: a pair of dazzling slippers, a floating house, a grown man in a lion's costume. But we were lucky, Olive and I; just as Norma beckoned us to follow her, a flashlight shone upon us. A movie usher, checking the theater. Olive froze. Norma froze. We sat back quietly into our seats, as if there were nothing to see here, nothing at all. I tucked my head back into the jacket as Norma whispered, "Five minutes, that's it. And then we're gone."

We stayed for the entire film.

The Wizard of Oz is really quite good, if you're in the mood for adventure. I wish I could tell you more about the film specifically, but I'm embarrassed to say that inside the theater it was dark and warm, with wonderfully soothing music trailing from the speakers. As much as I tried, I couldn't help nodding off, tucked cozily into Olive's overalls, listening to the *thump, thump, thump* of her human heart.

On Earth, I have thought about the future constantly.
How much of the universe would I fail to see if I lost my immortal life? How much would the hive miss my presence? And then there was the death bit—the actual, physical experience. Would it scare me? Would it hurt?

But I must say, during my first human lesson with Olive at the movie theater, I didn't think about the possibility of dying—not even once. When we were listening to Dorothy say, *There's no place like home*; when the lights flicked on and I yawned and stretched, pretending that I'd been awake all along; when Norma looked over at me and smiled, despite herself—these felt like livable moments, like I wasn't just going through the motions of being alive. I was *enjoying* myself, without the worry and the stress of thinking about what comes next.

As it happened, what came next was ice cream.

I know I have already mentioned ice cream, so forgive me if—for just a second—I retread old ground. Because this time it was much less about the eating and much more about the atmosphere. It was jovial. It was fun. And most of all, it involved Olive and Norma interacting in a way that I hadn't seen: like an invisible rope was strung between them, pulling them together.

"I feel like we just got away with something big," Norma said, laughing, as if she'd been part of our human lesson all along. A chocolate-cherry ice cream cone melted slowly in her hand. "Never in a million years would I think to do that."

Olive took another bite of her coconut ice cream, putting down the spoon. "Is that a bad thing?"

"Not at all," Norma said, finishing off her cone. "Your brain just works a little different. There's power in that. Now that Leonard's officially your cat, though— no one's responded to the posters I've put up—I think I have a right to know if you've got any other plans with him. No skydiving, mountain climbing, sneaking into the grocery store at two in the morning?"

"I think Leonard would like the grocery store."

Norma wiped her hands with a napkin until they were mostly clean. "I don't doubt it."

"And I . . . I might have promised him that we'd go bowling."

"Promised him?" Norma said, the corner of her mouth twitching into a smile.

Olive covered her tracks. "I mean, you know—I promised *myself*. That I'd take him. In a normal way."

An ocean breeze cut by our picnic table, swirling the humans' hair. A few crane flies dipped and dived behind us; Olive placed a hand over her bowl, just in case one got curious. At the same time, Norma squared her shoulders and said, "I'm glad that you and Leonard are becoming so close. I know it's—well, it isn't always easy making new friends."

"It seems easy for everyone else," Olive said, not impolitely—more like a statement of fact. "I just don't know how to be cool."

Norma chortled. "Sailor, you've got to be kidding me. I don't know *anyone* as cool as you. What other eleven-year-old knows about the transfiguration of ghost crabs, right off the top of her head?" She paused. "Did I ever tell you about my first time on a shrimp boat?"

Olive shook her head.

"Well," Norma said, "shrimping wasn't exactly a 'female' business. It was 'man's work.' That's what they told me, when I got my first job: that some of the crew might not take too kindly to it, working alongside a woman. *Especially* a woman of color. My sea legs were good, and I had a nice handle on when to drop the nets, when to bring them in. But I wasn't confident when people started talking about me, saying this and that. At first, I was so afraid of what they'd think of me—that they'd call me weird, or worse."

"Some people call me a weirdo," Olive admitted.

"Those are just people who haven't found out what they love," Norma said.

The two of them, they were having what humans call "a moment." While I was privileged to be a part of it, I almost felt as if I was intruding. Most cats might not acknowledge this—the human need for privacy— but I wasn't most cats. I gave them a bit of space, my leash extending into the grasses surrounding the picnic table. But as my nose followed several scent trails, I kept looking back at them: these people. This little family.

Olive made a funny noise with her throat, not quite clearing it. "Remember when I asked you about taking a trip? And you said we could go somewhere for a day?"

"Sure thing. Did you pick a place? How about Hilton Head?"

My chest clenched as Olive blurted it out, words blending into one. "How-about-Yellowstone?"

Norma quirked her head. "Yellowstone?"

"Yellowstone National Park."

"That's what I thought."

"Well," Olive said, "can we maybe . . . go at the end of the month?"

"Are you yanking my chain?" Norma asked, snorting out the words.

Olive winced. "I have some money saved up—in my piggy bank, under my bed at home. I could pay you back at Christmas. And I could do chores for you. Clean your motorcycle, or give Stanley a bath, or . . . or anything. Anything you wanted me to do. Every summer, and over the holidays, and—"

Norma flattened her palm to the air. "Hang on a second. Where's this coming from?"

"I . . . just want to go to Yellowstone to see the . . . you know, the bison."

"The *bison*? I'm not traveling halfway across the country for some bison."

"But they're . . . endangered?"

"What's this really about?" Norma said, losing her patience a little.

"I just want to go," Olive said. "That's all."

"Well. . ." Norma fidgeted, like her feelings were a bit hurt. Didn't it seem as if Olive was rejecting their summer plans? "It's out of the question. I have loads of work to do, the sea turtles are hatching soon, and we've got a good thing going on at the aquarium. You're having a nice summer, like I promised your mom. We're sticking to the schedule. Besides, even if we could go, where would we stay? I'm not even sure if my truck could make it that far. And my motor-cycle's out of the question, not for such a long trip."

"I just think—"

"You're not thinking," Norma said, cutting her off. "Because you're eleven, and you don't understand."

It was like the air froze and my fur was suddenly cold. But what could I do? Jump in and say something? Tell Norma that Olive was acting kindly on my behalf—that she understood more at eleven than I did at three hundred? No. No, that would expose me. But still, it was incredibly difficult to stomach the expression on Olive's face, her dimples un-dimpling.

She pushed away the rest of her bowl. "I'm not really hungry anymore."

"Then let's pack it in," Norma said.

So we went. And I wondered with an increasing sense of terror if—after this, after everything I was costing Olive—I'd get stuck on Earth after all.

22

The next day was uncomfortable, to say the least.
Everything was quiet. Quiet breakfast, quiet ride in
Norma's truck. On the way to the aquarium, Olive was
whispering to me, pointing out sights in Turtle Beach:
a stand for saltwater taffy, the little bookstore and its
window displays, the miniature golf course dotted
with windmills.

Norma just drove.

In the parking lot, she retied the bandanna around
her neck, straightening herself out. "Keep your wits
about you," she said as a reminder. "Today's penguin
day, so it might get a little wild."

This was very much the case. Four groups of sun-
burned tourists were waltzing through the shark
tunnel, and the gift shop was overflowing with cus-
tomers. They clutched their sea lion mugs, their faux

otter backpacks. Glistening bouncy balls thwacked against the cool tile floor. Norma, Olive, and I skirted through the crowd, deflecting comments from pass-ersby: "Mommy, Mommy, a cat!" "Hey, look, it's a kitty." "What in the—?"

You'd think they'd never seen a feline before! We were right by the jellyfish tank, too; I wasn't nearly the oddest creature in this place.

Finally, we saw Q, who shouted over the crowd, "How are you with penguins?" He was dressed in a wet suit, which is what humans call a constricting rubber tube with cylinders for arms and legs. I did not want one. It was the first time that I was relieved—well and truly relieved—to not wear an item of clothing.

He gestured to a door behind us. "There are some rubber boots in the back. I'm afraid I couldn't find any in Leonard's size, but yours should do. Suit up, partner! I'll meet you back here in five. Leonard can watch us from the window with Norma, if he wants."

"Watch us do what?" Olive asked, excitement creep-ing into her voice.

Q winked. "Guess you'll have to find out."

Penguins are not a species with which cats usually interact. Though there was an undeniable coolness to them—the way they ducked and dived and waddled. At the aquarium, they lived in a colony of twelve and spent a great deal of time swimming, lounging on the rocky shore, and eating bucket after bucket of anchovies. As Olive slipped into the back to change, passing my leash to Norma, I made my way to the exhibit area, letting the scent of salt guide us.

"What, you're not hissing at them?" Norma asked me, settling by the enclosure. A few of the penguins were pushing around a beach ball, and I couldn't stop staring at them, with their tightly packed feathers, their speckled bellies, brightness around their eyes. "I thought all cats hissed at birds."

It was the first time she'd spoken to me—really *to* me. The only thing I could think to do was rub the side of my face against her calf, my tail sky-high and jittering. This seemed the right response, because she bent down for a second, smoothing the fur of my back.

Olive and Q emerged soon after, wearing rubber boots and carrying buckets in their hands. Something about them was very much like Yellowstone rangers. They looked professional; in control of the situation. I hadn't realized that I could read lips, but I could see Q whispering to her: "You're doing great. Now, we've got a nice fishy breakfast for these fellas. All I got this morning was Frosted Flakes, but whew! They're lucky."

The penguins rushed over to Olive with quick waddles. She couldn't stop smiling as she tossed them sardines, anchovies, and squid. They ate eagerly with massive gulps: a much more efficient way to consume food. (Humans should take note.)

"She's a natural," Norma said to the air—and she was right. Olive looked at home out there with the animals, in her overalls and rubber boots. And it occurred to me, in that flash of a moment, exactly what I could do for her—how I could make up for the worry and the stress, her fight with Norma and the nights of staying up late, mapping out possible routes to Yellowstone. I was asking so much and giving so little.

Now, I would give.

Olive had told me once: *I'd do just about anything to have a conversation with a penguin.* Well, I couldn't give her that—not exactly. But I could already tell that the penguins were intrigued by me—their black eyes were flickering, wandering in my direction, and they were asking one another, *A cat?* One of them said: *No, no.*

Intelligent birds, indeed.

It didn't take terribly long to figure it out: their

system of braying and vocal communication is startlingly similar to a cat's, if cats were crossed with the common seagull. The key was in the throat, vibrating it just so, while throwing my head back at a sharp angle.

Which I did.

"Got a hair ball?" Norma asked, giving me a once-over.

Obviously I hadn't perfected the language *quite* yet. I tried again—much louder this time, with more full-throated action, my voice bouncing off the glass. And the penguins turned, away from the fish, away from Olive and Q. I had their complete attention.

It put me rather on the spot.

"What the—?" Norma said.

And I said, *Huuuh-huuu-huuuun-eeeee-oooo*, adding honk after extended honk until my message was clear. The penguins were resistant at first. I was a stranger, after all; we'd only just met. But it wasn't about me, I told them. It was about the girl.

"*Leonard,*" Olive mouthed to me, her cheeks flushing. "What are you—?"

The penguins pivoted, circling around her, until it was just Olive in the middle of them all. And then, all at once, they bowed in her direction, each lifting a flipper into the air.

Olive's face showed nothing.

Nothing and then—

She broke into a grin, clasped her hands over her mouth, and started to cry.

You'll have to forgive me if I'm getting a little emotional, but I'd very much like to keep this image. This is how I'd like to remember Olive, after I say goodbye to Earth: deliriously happy, tears of joy streaming down her human face.

I know it's just wishful thinking, though.

I won't be able to feel those memories at all.

So much for staying under the radar. My little stunt with the penguins was incredibly noticeable. Days later, Q was still bringing it up.

"I've never seen anything like that," he said, shaking his head as he squeegeed the tank glass. "Never in all my years. It's like . . ."

"Like . . . what?" Olive said cautiously, wringing her hands.

Then he shook his head again, brushing off the idea.

That Tuesday, Olive and I bought a gigantic paper calendar from the boogie board store. It had drawings of seashells in the corners and a shark announcing the days of the week. "This way we can count down," she said, as if I wasn't already numbering the hours. "I wish we could just leave now. But we have to plan the timing right. If we go too early, Norma and my mom will know I'm missing, and they'll come get me, and then you're toast. I'm not abandoning you with all those bears in Yellowstone. This gives us enough time to get there—*and* not get caught before you're picked up." We tacked the calendar low on the wall in Olive's bedroom, and she circled July 18, the night we'd leave for the park. Not long ago, I'd written ALIEN in this very spot.

"I'm still working on Norma," Olive said. "Maybe she'll come through, once the Save the Sea Turtles event's over. But I have some other ideas, too. You said your planet is made of helium, right? Maybe we could get a bunch of balloons, like in that movie *Up*, and fly them across the country? No, you're right— that's silly. And kind of impossible. How do you feel about the train?" After batting plans back and forth, we always returned to the same point: that we needed the help of someone who wasn't eleven years old.

"We'll think of something," Olive said. "I promise." But she was sounding less and less sure.

My tenth evening on Earth, I learned that most alien films aren't as kind to extraterrestrials as *E.T.* As we were flipping through channels, I meowed sharply, asking Olive to pause on a movie about the destruction of a city. There were tentacles in the background.

"Are you sure you want to watch this?" she asked, her eyebrows frowning in that human way. And I was. Incidentally, the film was part of a marathon: alien movie after alien movie. Explosion after explosion. Little green creatures tearing apart the world. *So this is what they really think of us*, I mused, eyes glued to the television. Eventually, Olive flicked off the screen, saying that we should relax on the porch swing instead.

"That's not how I see you," she said, rocking us back and forth. "I hope you know that. People are just afraid of what they don't understand." Her fingers fell across my fur, and I leaned into her palm, into her familiar scent: cinnamon toast and raspberry shampoo.

We spent most evenings this way, just the two of us. Some mornings, there were human lessons and the occasional errand. I visited my first "Walmart," a palace of human objects, where Norma bought peanut butter in bulk and Olive selected a new litter box: a fancy one, with an electric scooper. Only slightly less impressive were the gigantic plastic balls by the register; I'd seen planets smaller than those balls.

What was their purpose? Why did humans enjoy them?

The longer I spent on Earth, the more questions I had. For example, why was stubbing a toe so painful for humans? (It's a superficial appendage. There are nine others!) Was it truly necessary to floss? (If so, why didn't cats do it?) And why did everyone claim there was a man on the moon? (Didn't he get lonely, out there by himself? Might I suggest a cat for company?)

In between shifts at the aquarium, Olive let me practice my knock-knock jokes.

Knock-knock, I typed.

"Who's there?" she asked.

Leonard.

"Leonard, who?"

Just Leonard. It is me.

Olive laughed, then taught me Monopoly. In two weeks, I learned much about recreational board games: Battleship, chess, Hungry Hungry Hippos. I'm ashamed to say that I became mildly obsessed with those hippos, violently stamping the lever with my paws, little white marbles flying everywhere— and I chased them, underneath the sofa, across the living room.

We read poetry books, too: Walt Whitman and

Emily Dickinson, Robert Frost and Langston Hughes; we studied them by the shore, early in the morning, until I learned the simplicity of the haiku, the openness of free verse. Finally, I wrote a poem of my own.

"Can I see it?" Olive asked—and I shyly stepped aside from the computer keyboard, letting her read the stanzas aloud.

I have hidden
your crayons
in the litter box;

maybe you were
keeping them
for later.

I'm sorry;
they were so colorful
and so bold.

"You're a quick learner," Olive said, stifling a giggle. "Is this modeled after that William Carlos Williams poem? Or did you really hide the crayons in the litter box? Because I don't want to fish those out." I assured her that the crayons were safe in her desk—and then promptly dug them out of the litter, where I had in fact tucked them away.

Let's see. What else?

Q taught me how to high-five and called me several times over the loudspeaker at the aquarium: "Leonard to the front office! Leonard, office, please." Olive discovered the joy of snorkeling, slipping below the surface of the water in a stream of bubbles. And I became something of a mascot for the aquarium: people began to greet me by name. You may be familiar with a certain breed of human—the "cat lady"—but quite a few of them started showing up at the aquarium, posing with me, asking Olive to take our picture. Because I was easily able to speak the language of most creatures on Earth, I helped with aquatic care as well, telling Olive: *This one is sick; this one needs more food; this one is happy.*

Norma kept asking, "Sailor, are you psychic or something?"

And Olive would shrug, smiling.

"I'm going to help Q give an aquarium tour soon," Olive said one evening, right after dinner. "I actually get to talk about animals. That's what I'm *supposed* to do . . . I'm just not going to tell Frank about it." She closed the bedroom door. "I know it's selfish, but sometimes I really wish you were coming to Maine with me. Or California. Or just . . . anywhere. With people, there are all these rules, and they're not written down anywhere. With animals, it's easier. I mean, I guess you're not technically an animal, but you're still very friendly."

You are friendly, too, I typed.

"Thanks," she said. "But friendly doesn't always count in middle school. It's like being dropped on an alien planet."

Obviously, I knew what that was like—how it felt to wear ill-fitting fur, to look at humans from the outside, searching for a way in. Some nights, I'd watch Olive for hours: she would practice human phrases in the mirror, plucking at the ends of her hair.

"I'm Olive," she'd say. "Do you go to school here? Uh, of course you do. Let me start again." Then she'd start again. "It's Olive. Hi. Just Olive. I'm new."

The thought resurged in those moments, crowding out everything else: *Would it be the worst thing, to stay on Earth?* Yes, I was desperate to see the sunrise on my home planet; yes, I missed the all-encompassing safety of the hive. But would it be the worst thing, to be there for Olive when she came home from school? To actually use my electric litter box through its lifetime warrantee? To see Maine, to keep in touch with Stanley, to—

"What are you thinking about?" she asked, turning to me.

And I told her, **Say, Hello, I am Olive. Humans like hello.**

24

The next week was difficult for all of us. Norma was running around, trying to firm up details for the Save the Sea Turtles event, when two hundred guests would flock to the aquarium. Turtle Beach was already flooded with tourists, eagerly preparing for the weeklong festival. In the mornings, we watched them stroll through town, poking their noses into shops. In the evenings, I could always find Olive by her computer, searching train timetables, looking for used cat carriers, mapping out our route. It scared me—how wobbly our plan was, how quickly time was passing. Actually, scared is an understatement. People do that on Earth: try to tell themselves that everything will be all right, even if the evidence is against them.

No, a closer word is *panxious*, which I've come up with just now: a mixture of panicked and anxious.

You think I was petrified of noises before? That week, every little sound had me jumping. I accidentally scratched the hardwood in the kitchen after hearing a lawn mower; Norma's motorcycle boots squeaked and I flew off the couch.

"It's okay," Olive reassured me, stroking my back.

But it wasn't, not really.

Every once in a while, I'd catch snippets of conversations: Olive asking Norma to reconsider a trip to Yellowstone, Norma batting the suggestion away. Tension gripped the beach house, until it began to feel very small—and stuffy, like a backpack. Sometimes Olive would stay an extra hour at the aquarium, just mopping the same spots on the floor; and I wondered how her summer might've looked if I'd never shown up in that tree. Would she and Norma have flown kites in the cul-de-sac? Gone for bicycle rides? Picnicked by the shore?

Instead, Olive was giving human lessons to a cat. I'm sure you've been paying attention, but as a reminder, the list was as follows:

1. ~~Go to a real movie theater~~
2. ~~The creation and enjoyment of poetry~~
3. Bowling and ~~recreational board games~~

4. Preparation and consumption of a cheese
sandwich

5. Host a dinner party

Olive had been faithfully crossing off items, but occasionally she'd glance at the list, chewing heavily on her thumbnail. "*Bowling.* That's stumping me. Do they even make those shiny little shoes for cats?"

I very much hoped so.

"We're going to skip that for a moment and come back to it," she finally said, closing the laptop, and I trusted her to keep her word, even as time slipped away.

And it was slipping, very fast. Between board games and the beach, poetry and long days at the aquarium, it felt like I'd blinked and three weeks had passed.

Finally, we decided to combine the last two items on the list. Olive and I would host a cheese-sandwich dinner party—a simple affair, arranged tastefully on the beach. Naturally, I wanted to look my best. As a human, the outfit choice was obvious: a slim-fitting suit with a bow tie that popped. Or something more casual: a linen vest with a pocket square. But as a cat, I could hardly ask for another outfit—I had my raincoat, my collar, and my stingray T-shirt, all of which were appropriate for most occasions. I also had my fur—and that, unfortunately, needed work.

You may not truly understand how it feels to be greasy, for patches of your belly to turn slick and matted. The urge did strike me quite frequently: to lick myself, to lick and lick and lick until everything was fluffy and clean. But I hated how *animalistic* this was. It is not a dignified posture, to stick your leg in the air and bury your face into the crease of your buttocks.

Even Olive began to notice. "You're . . . um, missing some spots," she said, the morning of our dinner party. "I wouldn't say anything, but . . . you might be more comfortable if you cleaned them. I could also give you a bath? If you wanted?"

Well, that was completely out of the question. Sure, I might've enjoyed watching the water as it spritzed from the tap—miraculously flowing, drop by drop—but actually *submerging* myself in it? Never mind a rough towel or a too-hot blow-dryer with its sharp whirring noise. No. I would handle matters myself.

In the cool darkness underneath Olive's bed, I spent two hours on my leg patches alone. I dug my nose into my belly, grooming my midsection with gusto. And yes, my fur did begin to fluff in a more presentable way. The top of my head was most difficult to reach, as my tongue didn't extend quite that far. Eventually I learned to lick my paw *first*, then rub. (It didn't take me too long to discover this; we are, after all, a brilliant species.) Then I paced back and forth on the ridge of the sofa, and carefully pressed my nose to the window glass, waiting for Olive to return from the store.

"I grabbed cheddar," she said an hour later, setting the groceries on the countertop. "And Swiss. And Brie, Gouda, American, goat cheese, Muenster, and string cheese. I'm not sure what kind the string cheese is, but it's . . . Well, it has string in the name, so you'll like it. You think I got enough?"

Peering into the bags, I ogled the cheese with satisfaction. I couldn't really smell it through the thick plastic wrapping—and it all looked roughly the same color to my eyes—but this was still an important moment. I'd heard so many things about the charm of cheese, about humans delighting in the taste. Good things were surely to come.

Olive unpacked two loaves of bread—one sourdough, one wheat—then helped me wash my paws with soap and water. I flinched, whiskers bobbing, but she told me this was crucial. I couldn't contaminate the cheese with my litter paws.

Here is what I've learned about the art of sand-wich making. It is about more than shoving slices of cheese onto bread. It's about the sights and the sounds of the kitchen: the refrigerator humming, the curtains swishing with wind. It's about who you make the sandwich *with*—and the thought of enjoying it together. By the end, we had twenty-five sandwiches, neatly stacked.

"You know it's just going to be me, you, and Q," Norma said, entering the kitchen.

"And Leonard," Olive said.

She examined the sandwiches, lifting the bread. "You don't want to put anything else on them? No mustard? No pickles? We've got some lunch meat in the fridge."

"Just cheese," Olive said, packing the sandwiches in a wicker basket. Stanley decided at the last moment to join us in the truck—because there was food involved, and he was quite a fan of food.

The four of us drove with the windows down, the sun simmering low in the sky, the scent of salt tick-ling our noses: no matter where you were in Turtle Beach, you were never far from the ocean. Olive stuck one of her hands out the window, letting it swoosh in the breeze. From the back seat, I watched her—and something in me said, *I've known you forever*. Not just an earthly forever, but a deep sort of always, like I'd met her before even saying hello. There is an expression on this planet, that someone is an old soul. That they are wise beyond their years. I can tell you, without hesitation: this describes Olive perfectly. She may be only eleven, but her soul has lived and lived.

"Almost there," she said, as Norma turned down a rocky path, the water gleaming in the distance.

The whole thing was different from how I'd imagined. We did not spend the afternoon folding cloth napkins into elegant swans. There were no polished silver spoons, no glazed hams glinting under the light of a chandelier. But there was Q in a Hawaiian shirt, waiting for us by a sand dune, a six-pack of root beer in his hand.

"No party is complete without root beer," he said very seriously, then smiled.

Olive unfurled a picnic blanket on the ground and unpacked the sandwiches. "Thanks for coming."

"What, are you kidding me?" Q said, bending down to scratch my head. "I wouldn't miss this for the world. Not every day that you get to dine with the king of cats."

Norma snorted—but in a nice way, like Stanley laughing through the sprinkler.

We ate from paper plates. We spoke about the aquarium and the penguins. We watched the tide roll out, sloshing in waves. Nothing about it was fancy. I'm embarrassed to say that I didn't even like the cheese sandwiches. The bread stuck to the roof of my mouth; the cheese soured on my tongue. And halfway through the meal, my belly gently rumbled. I thought maybe my food was digesting improperly—that I was lactose intolerant after all—but then it began to travel: up, up, up through my throat. It burned slightly. I started to retch.

"It's okay," Olive said, concern in her voice. "It's probably just a hair ball."

Just a hair ball! I smarted at the word.

I won't go into any further details, because it really was too terrible to describe; let's say that I don't wish the experience on anyone. It itches. It burns. But afterward, the five of us dipped our toes into the sea. Olive rolled up her overalls and splashed in the water with Stanley, who shook his furry mass, droplets flying everywhere.

As for Q, he kept studying me, watching me with careful eyes. Eventually, his feet kicked through the sand, and he came to stand by my side. "You know," he said, "Olive told me that this dinner was for you. When you find someone who loves you like that, Leonard, you never let them go."

But I *would* have to let go—and soon.

I had four days left on Earth.

After the picnic, we strolled along the boardwalk.
It was early evening, the last bits of light dappling the
sea. Stanley was particularly interested in the cotton
candy stands, in the humans fishing off the pier.

Q and Norma trailed in front of us, chatting like
old friends do—and when they were out of earshot,
Olive pulled me quietly to the side, bending down
on the boardwalk. She said she had something to tell
me. "I've figured it out," she whispered, eyes glistening. "How we will get to Yellowstone. There's a
train station just outside of Turtle Beach, and if we
make the right connections, we can go all the way to
Salt Lake City, Utah. I called, pretended to be Norma,
and reserved a ticket as an 'unaccompanied minor.'
Then we take a shuttle to Yellowstone. We leave in
two days."

I was speechless. Olive was willing to put herself on the line—for me. She was bringing me to back to the hive: helping me to safety, to home; and for that, I owed her everything. It took a few seconds before I could pull myself together—emotion was flooding my chest—but I managed to purr, nudging my face against hers. *Thank you*, the gesture said. *Thank you for the plan.*

"Welcome," she said, understanding me perfectly.

The next hour came and went, the cheese settling in my stomach. Q purchased one of those pirate hats with the faux parrot on the side, and challenged Olive to a swordfight; they dashed along the sand, clutching dried stems of beach grass. Stanley continued his seagull hunt, stalking them on the shore. And Norma—Norma excused herself to take a phone call. I watched her with curiosity as she paced through the surf, her free hand carving the air.

It was a long phone call.

So long that Olive stopped beach-grass fighting, her silhouette illuminated in the dying light. "Who do you think she's talking to?" Olive asked Q.

Q appeared slightly worried, an expression I wasn't used to seeing on his face. His jaw tensed as he said, "Dunno."

We found out quickly enough.

Norma ended the call and stood there for a long moment at the edge of the shore, foam collapsing around her ankles. My first night on Earth, I was blown away by the sturdiness of her. Now, against the backdrop of the ocean, I couldn't imagine anything smaller. I could see Olive in her, in the lines of her face, the nimble stretch of her fingers. Finally, she trudged over to us—Q, Olive, Stanley, and me, waiting by an empty picnic table.

"You better sit down," she told Olive.

"What is it?" Olive said, voice quivering. "Is it bad? Did someone die?"

"No!" Norma said quickly. "No, no, nothing like that. Just sit down, will ya?" So we all did—even Stanley, snuffling through sand and crumbs under the picnic table. Norma inhaled a gusty breath. "That was your mom. She wanted to talk to you, but I said it was better to break the news in person. So here it is. Frank's been offered a new life-coaching job with an agency in Sacramento. It pays a lot more than his old gig, and your mom's got some leads on a new job, too. What I'm trying to say is . . . you're moving to California. And they're picking you up tomorrow night."

I stiffened.

Olive twitched with panic. "What? That's not— Wait. *Tomorrow?* My mom said she wasn't coming to get me until August."

Norma didn't look pleased, either. She kept loosening the bandanna around her neck, as if it were strangling her. "That was the plan. But things seem like they're moving quickly, and your mom misses you. She said this'll give you more time to get a fresh start in a new place, get you adjusted before school begins."

"But that's . . ." Olive said, beginning to tremble. "That's not fair. She promised!"

"We had a good run, didn't we?" Norma asked, words softer than usual. "A darn good run. Maybe you'll even come back next summer."

Olive stood. "I don't want next summer! I'm not done with *this* summer. What about the turtles? What about the tr—"

She paused, biting her lip. Because she almost said it: *What about the train?* I knew that Olive leaving for California had disastrous consequences for me. Would I go with her, not to Yellowstone? What about our ticket to Salt Lake City? But right then, all I could focus on was the pain sliding across Olive's face: how it was swallowing everything about her.

On the walk back to the car, Olive announced that she "needed a minute." The stars were beginning to pop into view, and I was wondering if I'd ever see them on my home planet again.

"We can wait right here," Q said, stopping by the seashell stand, "if you want."

"Go on," Norma said, bobbing her head at Olive. "It's okay."

Somberly, Q and Norma both dug their hands into their pockets, and I believe that Stanley would have done this, too—if he had pockets or hands. There was something rather sullen in the black curve of his lips, as he watched us disappear into the glittering darkness of the arcade. All around us were whirring noises, electric bells, shrill *pop*s. And the lasers! Don't even get me started on the lasers. Thin beams of light, racing everywhere. Nothing about the arcade helped my heart rate—and I don't believe it was doing much for Olive, either. She darted to the back corner, near the pinball machines, and started to pace, hands on her head. Her breath came unsteadily, matching my own.

The place was mostly deserted, except for a couple shooting a bouncy ball into hoops, so no one noticed when Olive blurted, "This is a total *disaster*."

I couldn't agree more. There was a numbness near my claws, as if the stress had traveled right to the tips of me.

"They couldn't have waited a few more days?" Olive asked. "Why'd it have to be *tomorrow*? I gave you my word, Leonard. I promised that I'd get you to Yellowstone—and the train was going to be really special. You know they have skylights and everything? We were going to eat in the club car and play I Spy out the window and—*ugghhh*." She let out a guttural sound, which rattled through me. I was trying hard to look at her, but the lasers were crossing my eyes.

"Now we can't do any of that," she said, voice cracking a little. "Now you might have to use a litter box forever and get stuck on Earth forever, and it'll all be my fault—because I promised you, I *promised* you." Her last words were so strained, I could barely hear them.

But none of this was her fault. None of it. It was mine.

Mine, I told her, pawing at my chest.

She didn't hear, didn't see.

Her hands tugged at the roots of her hair. "What are we going to do?"

And that, perhaps, was the most frightening thing of all. I had absolutely no idea.

26

It is my experience on Earth that events come in twos or threes. Try not to quote me on this—I'm still learning—but on the drive back to the house, as we were all reeling from the blow, a second phone call arrived.

At first, Norma seemed hesitant to pick it up.

She ignored it.

The phone rang again.

This time, it was Q—calling from his car. Norma put it on speakerphone, and his voice filled the space: "The sea turtles! They're hatching."

Norma gasped, then grunted. "I've still got Stanley and Leonard with me. Should I drop them off back at the house?"

"No time," Q said. "They're just going to have to watch from the sidelines. Turtle hatching is, without a doubt, the world's greatest spectator sport."

Olive piped up from the back seat. "What do I do?"

The smile in Q's voice was clear. "You, my friend, are going to help save some turtles."

And so we drove on, a coal-black sky gleaming above us. In terms of Earth towns, Turtle Beach isn't too large—just a few ice cream shops, a marsh, a library with a South Carolina flag shivering in the breeze. It took us very little time before we were swinging into another parking lot, a crowd already forming. Humans with red flashlights lit the way to the shore.

Olive led both me and Stanley along the boardwalk, a sense of anxious excitement all around us. In the distance, I could already see them in the moonlight: a dotted line, moving slowly across the sand. Q met us on the boardwalk, then guided us to a nearby picnic table, telling us to wait just a second; he and Norma scampered toward the nests. I perched on my forelegs, tail swishing through the sand—inching closer and closer to get a better look. Olive reminded me with a soft hand on my shoulder that I was a cat, a predator, and I needed to give them space. What you may not know about sea turtles is that they're incredibly fragile when they're young and fresh from the nest, when their eyes are barely open and the only thought in their minds is *sea, sea, sea*. Sure, Olive understood that I wouldn't hurt them, but the turtles would only smell the outer layer of me—so I stayed still.

Eventually, Q wandered back at a slower pace and told Olive, "I'll hold these guys. You go on ahead. Help them get to the water."

"How?" Olive asked. "I don't want to mess up."

"You won't. Promise. All you do is keep 'em in line, make sure they don't dart from the path—but don't touch them. Watch out for seagulls. The turtles will do the rest."

Obviously nervous, Olive nodded and then jogged over to Norma, who was on her knees in the sand, already guiding the hatchlings to the sea. And it was beautiful. I don't use that term lightly—but it really was: the little turtles shuffling across the sand until they reached the shuddering waves. Their shells were so thin, their flippers no bigger than one of my toes. *They must be terrified,* I thought. *They must be over-whelmed, like I was, at the beauty and newness of it all.* Indeed, it occurred to me as I watched them—as they trailed inch by inch across the beach—that they *were* Earth. That they were beauty and terror, wonder and danger. Was it better to live this way? To really *live*, to experience everything, the good and the bad?

Above all, they had each other.

Q told me, as we were standing there, "They only leave the nest in groups."

My heart swelled.

I have never felt more human than in that moment.

I have never felt *earthlier* than in that moment.

Q crouched to his knees, puffing out a breath. Something about his face told me that my good feeling wouldn't last long.

And I was right.

Because these were the next words he spoke: "Leonard, my man . . . I think I know what you are."

I thought I'd been stealthier. I thought I'd been more careful. What gave me away? The raincoat, the day with the penguins, the way I cleaned my belly—too awkward for a real cat?

"It was the computer," Q said, answering my question without even realizing it. "I saw you with Olive once, after I'd dropped you off. Forgot my keys on the porch, and there you were in the kitchen, clacking away. Not many cats know how to touch-type."

Moonlight pelted my back, my heart rippling like the tide. You might be able to imagine my panic at this point. No? Then let me elaborate. I felt completely exposed, entirely vulnerable, paws frozen in the sand. My tail hadn't puffed that much since the night of the storm, but there it was, prickling hair by hair. Q's eyes searched mine—not in a threatening way, not at all—but I was still unprepared for it. The correct etiquette escaped me.

Should I deny his words with a sharp hiss, or head-bonk him lightly on the nose, signaling that *yes, yes, it was true*?

"Whoa there, don't stress out," he told me, echoing what I'd once said to Olive: *I am an alien do not be scared.* "I'm not gonna hurt you. Promise. I've always believed in aliens—never been afraid. Ever heard of Roswell? Now *that's* some cool stuff. The deep sea, too. Plenty of aliens in the deep sea, I'm sure of it. Humans don't know even half of what's out there."

Stanley, perhaps smelling my worry, licked the crest of my skull, licking and licking and licking until I wasn't entirely sure that I had any fur left. I'm sorry to say that it did nothing to help the anxiety. In fact, dog saliva was now dripping into my eyes.

"You're still Leonard," Q said. "Me figuring it out doesn't change a thing. As far as I'm concerned, it's none of my business. I just wanted to say that you can come to me, if you ever need help. Earth can be a scary place for a—"

"Oh," Olive said, pulling up short. I hadn't seen her approach, hadn't even heard her footsteps in the sand. "What's going on?"

She asked the question, but she knew. Maybe she could tell by the look on my face, the way my eyelids were fluttering. To punctuate the moment, Stanley barked once—loud and piercing.

Q stood, sand stuck to his knees. "Well," he said matter-of-factly, "I was just letting the cat out of the bag."

I assumed that was a human expression, but I didn't understand it. My head was swimming. There were no backpacks anywhere, not that I could see.

"Sorry," Q said, "bad joke." Besides Olive, the closest human was easily ten yards away, well out of earshot, but Q still softened his voice to continue. "I figured it out. Not that I was really *trying* to figure it out—but the answer was there. To me, anyway. Leonard isn't like any cat I've ever met. Because he's not really a cat, is he?"

Olive shook her head, perhaps unable to push any words from her human mouth. "No," she said finally. "No, he's not."

Q nodded. "Okay, then."

"You believe me?"

"I believe both of you."

"And you don't think it's all in my head?"

"'Course not," Q said, taken aback. "I saw those

penguins with my own eyes. What kind of cat could get them to *bow*?"

Above us, a seagull squawked, and I nearly jumped from my fur. Not because I was afraid—but because I was concentrating extremely hard. I was listening to the conversation, where it was heading. Logically, I knew what came next.

Olive nervously jittered her fingertips. "He has to go home."

"What, he's worn out his welcome already?"

"No," Olive said, shaking her head. "No, I mean he *needs* to go home. He's not supposed to be in South Carolina at all. He's not even supposed to *be* a cat. And if I don't get him to Yellowstone National Park in the next four days, he'll be stuck here, in that body, forever. And he'll die. Eventually he'll die, and then it'll be my fault, and I've gotten us a train ticket and a shuttle ticket but the train doesn't leave for two days, and my mom's coming to get me tomorrow, which means I'm going to fail him and—"

"Whoa, whoa, whoa," Q said, and I was sure that we were thinking the same thing. *None of this is your fault.*

Olive bulldozed on. "His pickup point is Yellowstone. And if I'm leaving for California, I don't know how to get him there. Norma doesn't want to drive."

"Norma knows?"

"I couldn't exactly . . . figure out how to say it."

"That's probably for the best," Q said, scratching his chin. Something in his face was falling. "I think you're old enough to hear this, Olive, so I'm going to tell you. After your dad passed away in that car accident, your grandmother just about disappeared. For weeks, she locked herself up in that house of hers, barely showered, and stopped talking to almost everyone but me. She had to recalibrate her entire existence. There was a lot of darkness. I want to help keep her in the light. This has been a particularly light summer. I'm not sure you know how much it means to her that you're here."

Olive breathed a single word. "Really?"

"Really," Q said. "Now, I'd hate to see her go back to that place again, where she felt like the world didn't make sense. Don't get me wrong: I'm not saying that losing someone and finding out about Leonard are the same thing. Not even close. What I *am* saying is that Norma specifically told me: *I can't take another shock.* I'd like to respect that. I think that telling her 'Aliens are real and Leonard is one of them' might fall into the shocking category."

"That makes sense," Olive said, after digesting this

information for a long, long time. "What should we do, then?"

Once again, Q peered down at me, shivering in my raincoat, the fur of my tail half puffed. "You said that Leonard needs to get to Yellowstone by when?"

"July twenty-first."

"And your mom's getting here tomorrow night?"

"With Frank," Olive added, a bit under her breath.

"Well, there's two ways you can play this. You can go with them tomorrow night, and take your chances with Leonard. Or . . ."

"Or?" Olive said.

"Remember at the beginning of the summer, when I told you that some people take the roads and some people take the marshlands? This might be one occasion where we need those roads. I understand that you don't want to disappoint your mom. I've met her. She's a good person. But when something's this important, I think it's okay to bend the rules." Then he said the most wonderful words. "Leonard, my man, how do you feel about motor homes?"

28

"This is absolutely nuts," Norma said the next afternoon, clanking dishes into the sink. And I would have liked to tell her: *I know, we are leaving so quickly; we haven't even had time to bowl.*

Q leaned against his shoulder in the kitchen doorway, ankles crossed. "Don't worry," he said. "There will be plenty of places to stop along the way. Olive will love it—get that kid a proper education. Best thing to teach you is the open road. What else is summer for?"

Norma grumbled. "Her mom's getting here in ten hours. And you can't just take off on a vacation that you thought of last night."

"Educational adventure," Q corrected her.

"For Pete's sake! What about the aquarium? Two hundred guests are on their way."

"Taken care of. TJ and the rest of the crew are going to step up their hours, and we've just got a boatload of new volunteers for end-of-summer events. Plus, I have a bunch of time-off stored up. Been saving it for a rainy day."

"And I'm supposed to tell her mom—what? That she hasn't seen her daughter in almost a month, but that's okay. Her plans don't matter?"

"I wouldn't lead with that, no. But you *could* mention that we'll drop Olive off in California afterward. Just a quick detour—only two states in between. She'll still have time to settle in. So, you coming? It would mean a lot to Olive. And Leonard."

"Well, then, by all means, if it would matter to *the cat*." I was listening attentively by the refrigerator—and I will say that her words stung. Maybe she knew it, too; she threw a glance in my direction, an apologetic look in her eyes. Her nose twitched. "Sorry to drag you into this, Leonard."

Don't mention it, I wanted to say—because really, I was the sorry one. Who was bringing all the fighting into this quiet house, if not me?

"Okay, okay," Q said to Norma. "The truth?"

"The truth would be nice," Norma said.

"It's for the kid," Q said, "but it's also for you. Wait!

Hear me out. You haven't left Turtle Beach for three years. *Three years.* That's a lot of sightseeing to make up for. Plus . . . I've seen the way you look at that kid. Your granddaughter's moving all the way across the country, and I bet you'd like some extra time with her. So when Olive brought up the trip, I latched on to the idea. Remember how we always talked about trekking around Yellowstone? Come on, Norma. Don't break my heart."

I knew that Q was stretching the truth, bending it to fit. But I was grateful.

Giving them some space, I hauled myself across the living room and into Olive's bedroom, where she was stuffing an old suitcase with paperback books. "It feels really weird, packing up all my stuff," she said, then she winced. "How bad are they arguing?"

I did my best impression of a human shrug, lifting my shoulder blades up and down—which is actually quite difficult if you are a cat. And I peered around her room for almost the last time. Leaving the beach house was giving me a strange sort of melancholy feeling. This human home: I remembered so clearly, when I first arrived, dripping wet with floodwater—how blown away I was by every little thing. The toaster. Small toothbrushes in plastic holders. The flickering of the TV. Now I would miss even the turtle night-light, with its eerie green glow.

How much would I remember, really? Because memories are nothing, I realized, without a feeling attached. And that would be stripped away, as I traveled back. *Logic*, my species said. Logic above everything else. Feelings cloud the way.

"Do you want to pack anything?" Olive asked. "I'll bring your new litter box, your bowls, enough food for the trip, and of course your raincoat. But I still have some room in my backpack."

What else was there? I had no suitcase of my own, no socks to bring.

She opened the laptop, just in case.

So I typed, **I am ready.**

It occurred to me that I should leave something— something for Olive to remember me by. A keepsake. Nothing too big. What could fit snugly in the palm of her hand?

Norma and Q were still arguing in the kitchen, so I slunk past them with ease, stopping by the plant holders. With my nose, I sifted through the pebbles— through the black, gray, blue. Once, at the aquarium, Olive stopped by the penguin enclosure and told me a fact: that male Gentoo penguins would tirelessly search through piles and piles of stones, until they found the smoothest, most outstanding one. Then they'd present the rock to their intended companion: as an offering, as an expression of their soul. *To me, you are as flawless as this stone.*

Soon, I found it—the perfect blue pebble—and carried it back to Olive's room in my mouth. I heard her outside, rolling her suitcase down the driveway, so I set it carefully on her pillow. Hopefully she'd understand, whenever she arrived back here—no matter how far in the future.

Hopefully she'd remember.

Q knocked softly then on the bedroom door. "Guess it's time."

So it was. I said goodbye—to Olive's room, to the house, my green beach towel still hanging there on the porch railing, fluttering in the breeze.

❦

"That is . . ." Olive said.

And Q said, "I know."

In the driveway was the most magnificent human vehicle I'd ever seen: boxy like a bus but with an undeniable air of sophistication, a green stripe splashed across the side. We were gazing at the whole thing with reverence and awe.

"Nineteen sixty-nine Winnebago motor home," Q said, tapping the white paneling. "RV of dreams. Bought her off Big Rick—you know, of Big Rick's Crab Shack? Couldn't stand to see a beauty like this just taking up space in a garage. Needs to be on the open highway, wind in her face."

"It looks like a fire hazard," Norma said, popping up behind us. She was carrying an army-green rucksack, Stanley swishing his tail by her side. She stopped in front of Olive. "Two things. First, I don't know why this means so much to you, but Q's convinced me this is a good idea. Getting to spend more time with you . . . well, it doesn't sound half bad. Second, we're going to owe your mom one heck of an explanation. I've just left a voice mail on her phone, saying we're driving you to California instead of waiting for them to pick you up, but start thinking of good apology presents now."

"So you *are* coming," Q said.

And Norma mumbled, "Yeah, yeah," as she flung open the Winnebago's side door, disappearing noisily inside.

There was something about a road trip, something
uniquely *alive*. I couldn't quite put my paw on it—why I
felt so free, deep down—but suddenly we were cruising
along a flat track of highway, and everything was humming: the air-conditioning, the tires, Norma. Before
we'd even left Turtle Beach, Q had put Johnny Cash on
the radio, and now Norma was mumbling along.

"Careful!" Q said, a smile growing on his face.
"Might just have to break out my ukulele."

Norma guffawed. "You know, I've never hurled
myself out of a moving vehicle, but heck, I'd give it a
go. No ukuleles. No group sing-alongs. This isn't that
kind of road trip."

"Oh, I beg to differ," Q said, tapping the steering
wheel. "How about we let Leonard decide? Leonard!
Sing-alongs, yay or nay?" He tracked my reflection in

the rearview mirror as I nodded, discreetly dipping my chin. Stanley also gave his seal of approval with a tender *a-woo*, his breath hot and smelling of salmon.

Olive stroked his head. On her lap was an atlas of the United States, and she was hunched over it, eyes tracing our route. "I'm not seeing much," she said above the music. Norma had suggested that she find some roadside attractions, short stops to break up our journey, and the idea thrilled me—that I might encounter a greater slice of humanity; the best that Earth had to offer.

"The world's largest rocking chair?" Olive said. "No, that's too far out of the way. Hmm . . . there's just a lot of Walmarts and—wait. There *is* a zoo. But Leonard and Stanley probably wouldn't be allowed in. And it's ten miles off the highway."

"Ten miles is nothing," Norma said, swiveling in the passenger's seat. "What's the rush, sailor? We can spare a couple of hours."

To this, Olive said nothing. I understood why. From Turtle Beach to Yellowstone was 2,329 miles, give or take a few, which didn't leave us with much wiggle room. If we traveled all day for three solid days, we'd make it just in time. No major stops. No extended bathroom breaks. It was a delicate balance; we'd have to rush without *looking* like we were rushing. Otherwise, Norma might start asking questions like: *Why do we have to be there by July twenty-first at 9:01 a.m.?* Already, the tension was building, and I couldn't help but yawn, my tongue curled, hoping to relieve the pressure. At the beginning of the month, I'd traveled across the universe on a beam of light—and this was more stressful by far.

It was also more enjoyable.

Together, Olive and I explored the motor home: we rolled back and forth on the springy bunk beds, searched the nooks and crannies for lost quarters, played cards at the small kitchen table. Well, Olive played cards—and I watched her flick the deck, so skilled with her human hands. Every two hours or so, we'd stop at a gas station and stretch our legs, Q buying stale French fries, Olive sipping from a wild-cherry Slurpee. Norma was meticulous about scraping all the bugs from the windshield, and I—resting on the dashboard—observed the squeegee with intense interest. It left streaks like shooting stars.

You could say that everything was going smoothly, according to plan.

Until we reached Asheville, North Carolina, and Norma insisted that we stop for biscuits.

"Not just any biscuits," she said. "The best dang biscuits you've ever eaten. Turn left here."

"Shouldn't we wait until Tennessee?" Olive suggested, trying to keep up the momentum. She offered Norma a bag of potato chips. "Here, I grabbed these for you at the last stop."

"Nuh-uh," Norma said, adamant. "These biscuits are from the famous Tupelo Honey café. They're an educational experience. That's what we're doing here, right? Don't be so worried about the time. A good biscuit's worth waiting for."

No one contradicted her.

So we turned off the highway, in the direction of breakfast pastry.

Perhaps this would have been fine—if it didn't happen again in the Nantahala National Forest, when Norma insisted that we take a long walk among the pines. "I'm not young like you," she explained to Olive. "I've got to stretch my legs every once in a while." Then, somewhere in east Tennessee, we lost half an hour to a farm stand, Norma picking over the fresh vegetables.

"We don't need *cucumbers*," Olive whispered to me. "We need to be on the road."

I tried to reassure her with a headbutt to the shins,

but the truth was, Norma's dillydallying was making me shed. Maybe it was just a side effect of summer, but by Tennessee, I was losing so much fur, it appeared that I was cloning myself. A Leonard here, a Leonard there.

"You can use my brush," Olive said sympathetically, then unloaded our stuff.

We stayed the night at a campground in Nashville—590 miles from Turtle Beach. It had a small pool that glittered under the moon, and several barbeque pits that left a strong scent of meat products in the air. Next to the Winnebago was a sun-bleached thicket of grass; in this, Q set up a circle of folding chairs—and whipped out his ukulele.

Norma protested.

Olive won.

"I could use a good song right now," she said, and who could argue with that? Jumping on a chair, I wrapped myself into a comfortable ball, my fur shimmering in the light breeze. So I had a front-row seat to what happened next: the way Q began strumming chords, how Olive started bobbing her head back and forth.

"All summer," Q said, "I've been thinking, you know what? Turtle Beach Aquarium needs a theme song.

Absolutely it does. If tourists hear a catchy tune on TV, something good and cheesy, they'll stop right in." He was joking—you could tell by the playful grin on his face—but Olive caught on quickly.

"Come by to Turtle Beach Aquarium," she sang. *"Where the sharks are cool, and the fish are—"*

"Scary-um," Q added.

Olive quirked her head. "'Scary-um'?"

"I know they're not scary, but just go with it," he said, then sang in a deep-throated gurgle: *"You'll have a blast, and time flies fast—"*

"When you're spending it with aquari . . . fun," Olive finished.

Everyone agreed that it was a dreadful song. But we were laughing. We were laughing under a moonlit sky. And in that moment, it was difficult to imagine anyone in the universe but us.

I fell asleep that night in the crook of Olive's arm, half beneath a patchwork quilt. I dreamed of Turtle Beach. I dreamed we were on the sand again, with the sea turtles, leading them to the water. But in the foggy distance, I felt it—time slipping away.

Only two days left, I woke up thinking. Two full days on Earth.

Stress tumbled in my belly, and I realized I'd shed a good deal in the night; there was a fuzzy outline where I'd slept. My fur looked greatly worse for wear, standing in pathetic tufts around my neck.

Olive was beginning to stir as Norma rummaged for mugs in the kitchen, the musky smell of coffee filling the motor home. "Is something wrong with Leonard?" Norma asked a minute later. She'd poured herself a strong cup and was glancing at me with her head askew.

Olive sat up on her elbows, grimacing at my fur. "He's . . . I guess he's tired?"

"Whatever he is, it's making him rough around the edges." Norma said this between glugs of coffee. "You think he could be carsick? We could take longer breaks if he—"

"No!" Olive responded, too quickly. She had to reel back the word. "I'm sorry. It's just that Q and I were talking about traveling a lot today. Seven hundred and fifty miles." With care, she smoothed the fur on my bib, where the tufts were spikiest. "Maybe we should take him to breakfast with us, though? Keep an eye on him?"

"Bring him to the diner?" Norma asked, at the same time Q popped from the bathroom and said, "Sure, let's take Stanley, too."

As the humans debated this, I took a moment to clean myself, trying to salvage the sleekness of my fur, and then we were off to the restaurant, a half mile from the campsite. It was a strange sort of earthly invention: a diner dedicated to the cowboy boot. Food delivered on cowboy-boot platters, cowboy boots pinned on the walls. What was the purpose of it all? And why was it so loud? The hostess gave Stanley and me a triple glance before leading us to a booth, where I was careful—very, very careful—not to scratch the vinyl seats.

When the waitress came, she scrunched her nose, eyeing us up and down, as if searching for fleas. "Um, sorry. But, like, we don't allow animals?"

If that was indeed true, why was she phrasing it like a question?

Q jumped in. "These aren't just any animals. This is Leonard, King of Cats, Champion of the Aquarium. And this is Stanley, who might be the size of a bear, but is, in fact, not one."

"Yeah," the waitress said, "I'm going to have to ask you to leave."

It was Norma who saved us with six simple words: "We'll give you a huge tip."

The waitress rolled her eyes but miraculously took our order. Olive selected pancakes for herself, half a scrambled egg for me; I rolled it in the smallness of my mouth, trying to savor the taste. Normally, I would have liked the egg: the savory quality, the way it folded against my tongue. But my stomach continued to tumble.

"Good thing I'm trained in the Heimlich," Norma said, watching Olive scarf down her pancakes. "Slow down, sailor. You'll hurt yourself."

"Sorry," Olive said, talking around a mouthful of pancakes. "I planned about twenty-seven minutes for breakfast, and it's already been eighteen."

From the floor, Stanley asked if anyone was going to finish those strips of turkey bacon. *They smell delicious*, he said. Unfortunately, I was the only one who heard him.

Norma stuck a fork in her hash browns. "You know, in my day, everything was slower. We used to play games to pass the time on car trips. Now, I'm not a big games person, but I'd be willing to, this one time." She sounded hopeful, actually. Grandmotherly.

Olive considered this. "What kind of games?"

"Anything." Norma shrugged. "I Spy. Twenty questions. Tic-tac-toe."

So, after we finished our meals and hurried back to the RV, Q suggested a game. "It's called 'Best Day on Earth.'"

"Never heard of it," said Norma.

"That's because I thought of it right now," he said, backing out of the parking lot before gunning the gas. We jerked forward, pulling onto the highway with a plume of exhaust. "You have two options: You can tell us about your best day on Earth, or you make up what you'd *want* your best day to look like. Leonard, you start." My eyes widened as he tossed a look back at me. "Kidding," he said. "I'm kidding! I'll go."

"Well, hold on a second," Norma said. "I've got one."

Outside, the streets of Nashville were blurring, and the rush of the air conditioner was flitting my fur back. I settled next to Olive on the built-in couch, listening. The world became very quiet, until all we could hear was the hum of the vents, the hush of tires against road.

Norma wrung her hands, turning to face Olive, Stanley, and me. She seemed to be debating something, her eyes glassy and flickering. "This story," she finally said to Olive, "is about your daddy. I guess I could say what I was *going* to say, which is some nonsense about riding my motorcycle to Canada, but I figure you deserve the truth." She tilted her chin upward. "To start with, the shrimp industry in South Carolina was collapsing. It was chaos. The catches were too sparse, too inconsistent—and we couldn't compete anymore, not with the Gulf of Mexico. People were ditching their boats left and right. I was one of the last locals to hold on, in the water with my crew, just pulling up air."

Norma's tone was grim, and Olive shifted uncomfortably beside me.

Q cut in, "And this is your *best* day?"

"Hold your horses," Norma said. "I'm getting to it. Now, on the day before I sold my boat, your parents came to visit me, sailor. You're too young to remember this—you were just a baby, a real little kid—but that's when I met you for the first time. I was in a horrible mood. A kick-the-world mood. But seeing your face, well, it faded away just a touch. And we went out on the boat: got a tiny life jacket for you, took out the trawler with your parents. I've never seen your dad happier, out there on the cove. Calm waters. The sun setting over the pier. It was beautiful—picture sort of stuff. But he kept his eyes on you." Norma's throat trembled as she prodded the area right above her heart. It took her a moment to continue. "And that's my best day on Earth."

I peered up at Olive. She had water in the corner of her eyes, and I could tell that words were failing her. She was breathing slowly, purposefully, like she was trying very hard to inflate her lungs. I wanted to console her, to breathe for her, because it was hitting me for the first time—hitting me in the most unexpected way—just how much Norma must miss her son. How much Olive must miss her father. All I could do was offer her a long, unblinking stare, my eyes half-slits. For cats, there is no greater gesture.

"Well, shoot," Q said, breaking the silence. "I was about to tell you about the time I met Jimmy Buffett in Margaritaville, but that's a no-go now. Doesn't seem serious enough." He drummed his fingers against the wheel. "Okay, here's one. You all know Teddy the dolphin? The team brought him in last week? Man, I've never seen an animal with injuries like that. Never. First couple of days, I didn't even think he was going to make it. But he's a fighter. He really is. And when he's ready to return to the ocean, I want to be there on the shore, toasting him with a bottle of root beer. That'll be my best day on Earth."

I shook my fur in agreement; that would be a good day, indeed.

A few raindrops pattered the windshield as Q told Olive, "You're up, kid."

But Olive was lost in her thoughts—even after Stanley and I nudged her. Even after Q said *you're up* again. All she did was stare out the window, watching the clouds flicker by.

⸎

Earth, by nature, is incredibly stormy. Tsunamis crash into cities. Tornadoes whip through cornfields. And walls of rain hit highways in rural Tennessee. Olive was still gazing out the window as the storm came, swiftly and suddenly. Our motor home began to swerve against burst after burst of wind. Water started pounding the roof, loud enough to make us jump. Part of me thought that it was fitting: I'd arrived on this planet with a flood, so why not leave with one?

Q voiced the other half of my thoughts. "Bad luck," he said, speeding up the windshield wipers. "*Bad* luck. I'm trying, but I can barely see a thing."

"Pull over," Norma instructed. "This isn't worth it. We'll wait it out."

"No!" Olive blurted, the first thing she'd said in an hour. Frantically, she consulted the map. "We need to keep the pace up, if we want to get there two mornings from now. It's still seven hundred miles to Lincoln, Nebraska."

"I'm sorry," Q said. "I really am. But we're not making good time in this rain, anyway. And if we get into an accident . . . That'll lose the *most* time. Storms are funny things; they sweep in, sweep out. You'll see. We'll be back on the road quickly."

Except it didn't happen quite that way.

At the next exit was a rest stop, and we waited there—first in the Winnebago and then at a covered picnic table, watching the rain glisten and fall. Lightning arrived: big bursts that split the sky. Stanley wasn't a great fan of lightning. Two flashes later, he was cowering beneath the table, fur bristling on the back of his neck. I scooted next to him, offering company and commiseration: *On my planet,* I said with my eyes, *there is no lightning.*

And he said, *Please, oh, please, make it stop.*

Little streams of water were seeping around us; I was flicking my paws, freeing them of droplets, when Norma asked, "You want something to drink while we wait? Thought I saw a vending machine just down the way." Q requested lemonade, Olive asked for chocolate milk, so Norma wrenched up the hood of her coat, slipping behind a sheet of water. It didn't take long before the storm consumed her completely.

Q drew a damp pack of cards from the pocket of his cargo pants. "You know, your grandma used to be a storm sailor. I've seen her go out when the waves were"—he whistled, pointing to the ceiling—"way up there."

"Really?" Olive said.

"Why do you think she has that motorcycle?" Q asked, shuffling the deck. "Still has some daredevil in her. Now pick a card, any card."

Olive selected a card from the bottom of the stack as I shook my fur. "I'm starting to get worried," she said. "The GPS says we have to travel eleven hours and nine minutes today, and that doesn't include bathroom breaks. Or snack breaks. Or storm breaks. Or Norma breaks. Do you think we could drive through the night? Is that possible?"

"Anything's possible with enough coffee," Q said, placing the cards on the table. "I could ask Norma to drive some. Her night vision's sharp as a bat's. But she'll ask why we're rushing."

Olive's shoulders drooped. "Yeah, that would be bad. You really think that it would shock her, telling her about Leonard?"

Q shuffled the deck once more, Olive's card somewhere in the middle. "My guess is yes. And I'd hate to risk it. Your grandmother's the best friend I've ever had . . . Now, important question," Q said, tugging a two of hearts from the deck. "Is *this* your card?"

Olive shook her head.

"How about this one?" Q asked.

"Sorry," she said.

"Well, darn," he said, half at the cards, half at the sky. The rain kept bolting down.

By the time we were back on the road, we'd lost
two and a half hours and Olive couldn't stop jiggling
her legs, or sitting on her hands, or pressing her forehead to the window, willing the motor home to move
faster. Nervously, I watched her from my perch on the
kitchen counter, a dishcloth draped over my back; it
wasn't nearly as cottony as my green beach towel, but
I was making do under the circumstances. My fur was
pitifully soaked.

Outside it was still misting. Norma opened several
windows anyway, allowing a foggy breeze. Between
gas-station snacks and Stanley's wet-dog scent, the
Winnebago was beginning to smell stale. We said
nothing to one another for over a hundred miles—just
let the wind do the talking.

In Nebraska, we finally pulled into the campground well after midnight, the RV chugging to a stop.

"*Whew,*" Q said, yanking up the parking brake.

"You said it," Norma added, stretching her back.

And Olive whispered that she had a surprise for me, if I wasn't too exhausted. She dug out her suitcase. Underneath a stack of books—the Whitman and the Wordsworth—there was a small green tent. "I bought it at a used camping store online, so I'm not expecting great things, but it should fit us both."

I like to think that my tail said it all—that Olive knew exactly how much this meant. It really was extraordinary, setting up camp in a lush bed of grass, not too far from a silver-topped lake. Inside the green fabric, I was a *ranger.* I was camping in the wilderness, the earth at my feet.

All that time, all that study.

And now, someone to share it with.

Olive brought out pillows, sleeping bags, and her laptop from the RV, and we settled in for the night, a flashlight between us.

"Eight hundred and ninety-two miles left," she said to the tent ceiling, her words sifting through the dark. "And we have to drive that in a *day*. It'll take us fourteen hours, at least. That's if we don't make any stops at all. We should've left earlier, Leonard. I should've figured everything out sooner. I'm so sorry."

She was apologizing to me? After all the good she'd done?

It occurred to me then: Olive could've had a regular cat. Maybe in an alternate universe, in another summer, that is what Olive found: an earthly cat, who'd curl up at the edge of her bed, day after day, year after year, until its fur grew thin and gray.

Instead, she got me. And I felt a bit ashamed, for not fulfilling that role. For bringing her on such a difficult journey.

"I really wanted to you to be my cat," she said, as if reading my mind, "and maybe a tiny part of me waited until the end of the month because I didn't *want* you to leave. Sometimes I wish that I could stay—that *we* could stay—in Turtle Beach forever."

I cocked my head at her. Turtle Beach, I understood; but I couldn't fathom why she wanted me so badly. On the surface, dogs seemed like much more reliable pets. They were obedient and loyal. They brought in newspapers. They attacked intruders in a more convincing manner than cats.

I pawed at her, asking, *Laptop, please?*

She rolled over to open it.

These were some of my last chances to ask her anything—ask her everything and anything on my mind. My raincoat swished as I typed.

Best day on Earth. That is a question for you.

"My best day?" she asked. "That's . . . Well . . . Can I tell you something first?"

I nodded.

"I've been thinking about what Norma said all day, about my dad. I can't *stop* thinking about it." Absentmindedly, she unclipped and reclipped her daisy barrettes. "I really did want to like my mom's boyfriend, Frank—to have someone else in my life. Not a dad, but someone *like* a dad. Someone in my corner. I mean, my mom's been there. Before this summer, the longest we'd been apart was for two weeks, when I was at Science Explorers camp. You'd like her a lot, Leonard. But lately she's always around Frank . . . and now he's going to live with us? Permanently? In *California*?"

Her nostrils flared as she blew out a breath. "I don't even know if he'll let us put up the photos. Of my dad. We keep a few on the mantel, a few in the kitchen. My dad loved to cook." She paused, hesitant. "Would you maybe want to see a picture?"

I did. I would. Before I could properly answer, though, she was reaching deep into the pocket of her overalls. I cannot tell you what that did to me, the realization that she was keeping him with her, all this time. It was a small photo, easily cupped in her palm, and there he was: rounded ears, light-brown skin, a gap-toothed smile. So much like Olive.

"I know people always say this in movies," Olive whispered, "but the worst part is, I don't even remember if I said goodbye. I don't remember much about him at all." She drew the sleeping bag tighter around her, and I readjusted myself, kneading the puffy fabric. "Leonard?"

I looked at her with a purr.

"When you leave, can you say goodbye?"

She said it so earnestly, so quietly, that it nearly stopped my heart.

"A real goodbye," she continued, producing something else from her backpack. It was a tiny circular object: flat, possibly cardboard, and yellow. "I know you're not dying or anything. It's the opposite. But . . . still." The corners of her mouth curled into wistful smile. "Sometimes I thought that if I had just one good friend—one really *good* friend—it would make all the difference. And then I met you. And it did."

In that instant, I understood what was in her hands. A ranger badge. A handmade ranger badge, with my name printed in black ink.

"We were supposed to get something like this in Girl Scouts, to go across our sashes, but I never got that far. So . . . I wanted to make sure you had one." Olive cleared her throat. "For bravery and resilience, and for excellent penguin communication, I award you the Yellowstone Badge."

She pinned it on my raincoat.

My throat quivered.

"You don't have to say anything," she told me. "I know."

We left the campground just before the crack of dawn. It was a long drive through the rest of Nebraska—nothing but rolling plains, dotted with the occasional tree. Everything was the color of tumble-weeds, and gigantic sprinklers spread across the fields like wings. As I stuck my head out the window, I found myself missing the beach, missing the sea grass and the shore.

There wasn't much time for stopping—the hive would collect me in less than twenty hours—but we ran low on gas in the middle of Nebraska, pulling into a station for a refuel. Norma tried to dawdle, perusing the gas station's aisles in an incredibly slow manner, while Q filled up the tank. Olive, Stanley, and I were waiting on the curb when we glimpsed something in the distance. Something moving.

"See it?" Olive asked.

Stanley *a-woo*ed in response, and I shuddered my tail.

It was standing a hundred feet away, just beyond the motor home. A deer with a white tail, her head dipping to chomp at a sprig of grass, her ears twitching in the mid-July heat. For a second, her gaze fell on the three of us, and it felt like a sign: that I was so close to the wildlife of Yellowstone, so close to leaving all of this behind. Because I wanted to leave tomorrow morning. And I didn't. The two were mixing in my mind—and continued to mix, as we played cards. As we listened to music. At the edge of Wyoming, clusters of trees trailed into forests. And I tried to hang on to each of these moments, these last moments, while I could.

Which brings us here.

That's it now. I've told you everything. Perhaps I've left out some details, bits and pieces here and there; if so, please forgive me. I only have nine more hours on this planet.

"Very good," Olive tells me, as I lick the crunchies bowl clean, my tongue scraping the smooth bottom. And I look up at her, always at her—the center of our story. I will miss the way Olive clacks her tongue when she's thinking. And Norma's terrible cooking, which I never quite learned how to chew. How is it possible that I will remember how Q whistles when he cleans the aquarium tanks, but I won't remember how it made me *feel*?

Outside are ghostly shapes, moonlit mountains. Earthly things. In my gut, I know—despite my adoration for this family, for these people—that I don't belong here. I'm an immortal being in a mortal body. I am not cut out for this.

A sign flashes by: YELLOWSTONE NATIONAL PARK, 1 MILE. My heart somersaults. We've almost made it after all.

Olive reaches down to smooth the top of my head, where the fur is spotted with black, white, and brown. For a second, she playfully lifts my paw up and down— hoping to distract me, maybe. Then she just holds it. Holds my hand.

I do not take it for granted, as humans so often do.

I close my eyes, letting myself feel.

She's taught me so many things on this planet: the names of marsh plants, like duckweed and cinnamon fern, black gum and arrowwood. She's taught me that there is something lovely about curling up on the porch, in a warm patch of sun, the marsh grass gently fluttering. All it takes, she's taught me, is one good friend.

In the front of the Winnebago, Q is cruising through the park's southern gate, fingers tapping the wheel.

Norma is cleaning mud off her boots, Stanley at her feet.

And soon, Olive is asking me a question. "I don't really get how it works," she whispers. "I mean, how do you like—*whoosh*? Get back into space? Travel up there?"

Away from Norma's view, Olive reopens the laptop, screen glowing in the dim light. The RV is swerving slightly; it's difficult to type, but I manage the words: I must go into the geyser.

"I'm sorry," Olive says. "What?"

You must help fling me into the geyser, I clarify. It is a hot spring named Old Faithful, which boils and erupts in a tall shoot of water. This will catapult me into the air. My species will collect me from there, counteracting the Earth's gravitational pull. Olive is still staring at me, eyes wild, so I add: I thought I had mentioned this.

"Oh my god," she says. "No, you didn't. How are we going to—?"

That's when the tire bursts, fifteen miles from Upper Geyser Basin. It's an oddly melodic noise: the *dugga-dugga-dugga* of metal on tarmac, sparks flying in fiery arcs, scattering across the road. The motor home veers violently to the left.

"Everything's fine!" Q says, trying to control the situation. His hands tightly grip the steering wheel. "Just a flat! We'll pull over and have it fixed in no time."

He sounds genuinely hopeful, and this eases my fear. Fifteen miles to Old Faithful is easy; we could walk there if we need to. What else could go wrong?

The Winnebago slows, edging to the side of the road, which is muddy from last night's rain.

"Why don't you take Leonard for a short walk, let him stretch his legs?" Q asks Olive, as Norma grabs a tire iron from the back. "I promise, this really isn't a biggie. I know it's after midnight and we're all exhausted, but I've changed *many* a tire in my life."

I can help, I try to tell him, pawing at my raincoat. Inside Yellowstone, I should be able to perform some of my duties as a ranger—assisting this family in distress; yet I'd like to help without damaging my raincoat, if possible. It's been pristine for my whole time on Earth, no mud or rips or tears.

"Are you too warm?" Olive says, noticing my

pawing. She peels the raincoat off my back and holds it in her arms, leaving me with just a harness and a collar. Stanley's on a leash as well, sniffing the grass beside Norma, his wet nose twitching against a tapestry of scent.

When his gaze tilts up again, he tells me, *The birds.*

Yes, I know, I reply, because he's been saying this for ages. Since I first met him.

The birds! he repeats, emphasizing his words with a yelp.

I don't truly understand the depth of Stanley's obsession with birds. Sometimes his paws twitch in sleep, and I wonder if he's chasing them. He's a reserved sort of dog, with a calm character. But whenever he glimpses a bird, everything about him perks up: his tail, the fur on his spine, the soft fold of his ears.

Which is exactly what is happening now.

"What is it, boy?" Norma says, handing Q the tire iron.

Stanley tugs at his leash, following a scent into the nearest bush. All I can see is the fluff of his back legs, the swish of his tail. His muffled bark rings through the branches. *No, not there,* he finally says, extracting himself from the bush. *There! Bird!*

Based on his reaction, I expect to hear the

thunderous flapping of wings. My ears swivel, whiskers flattening. I hear nothing. But something in me still ticks awake: some evolutionary response, buried within my earthly body.

I crane my neck to the sky.

Above me—etched in moonlight—is an enormous owl.

Olive had told me about the owls of Wyoming, which feed on small animals and perhaps the occasional house pet. I'm instantly mesmerized by the sharpness of its beak, the length of its claws, how it's screeching and swooping—circling around me. I don't even have my raincoat for protection: no slick layer of fabric between those talons and my fur.

The bird lets out a sharp cry.

And then it snatches my raincoat, right from Olive's arms.

It just glides down and steals it, carrying it away into the woods. My *raincoat*! With my Yellowstone badge! There are treats in the pockets and everything.

"What just . . . ?" Norma says.

"Hey!" Olive says, breaking into a sprint after it. Of course, I scamper by her side, my stride long, my paws barely touching the ground. Stanley howls. Really and truly howls. He pulls so hard on the leash, it drops from Norma's hands. His eyes are intensely alert, his paws mud-flecked as he stamps the ground—*thud, thud*—until he's chasing the owl alongside us. It's darting through juniper trees, my yellow raincoat dangling from its talons.

It should occur to me that this is dangerous. That this is foolish. Not too far away is the sound of rushing water. The earth is already wet and splintering beneath us.

But that's my raincoat, with my badge.

I want it with me to the very end.

The owl changes course, flitting sideways, and we skitter around a bundle of pines, trying to close the gap. Flecks of spittle are forming in the corners of Stanley's mouth. He won't stop barking. Norma won't stop shouting.

We crest the hill in a single, pulse-pounding moment. I stagger, my paws slipping in the slick mud, and I try to grip on to the tangle of weeds, the spongy layer of moss. No use. It's no use. Our feet are running faster than we can catch. The three of us—Stanley, Olive, and me—slide forward. Slide down.

It doesn't even matter when the owl drops the raincoat.

Because Olive is falling, her ankle twisting on

clumps of thistle—bending more as she tumbles along the rocks. Before I can stop her, warn her, *help* her, she skids into the river with a terrible gasp, her body smacking the water. Stanley has managed to dig his paws into the hillside, and we shriek together as Olive slips below the surface. The sound is raw in my throat, raw in my ears. Everything is *ringing*—and it's two seconds, three seconds before she resurfaces, black hair slick against her forehead. She's breathing in great gulps.

Barely afloat, arms flailing, she yelps out a word: "Leonard!"

It echoes through the forest. Echoes into me.

The birds! The birds! Stanley is saying, over and over again. Now I understand, now I really do, that he's been trying to warn me about birds all along.

Drawing upon my memories from the summer—Olive dunking under tanks, Q swimming in the ocean—I rise on my haunches, catapulting off the shore and into the river. No, cats aren't designed for swimming; the water reminds me with its coldness, with the heaviness of its current. My little white paws flit pathetically beneath me as my tail struggles to find something to do. Should I use it as a dolphin might? Or a sea otter, propelling myself through the water? I try to imagine that my toes are webbed, that the water is warmer—that I am, most of all, unafraid.

Olive matters more than anything else.

My lungs flatten when I realize that I've lost sight of her. I blink wildly, unable to wipe the water from my eyes. Everything about me swivels—my ears, my body. I'm turning and turning in the water; if I listen hard enough, paddle close enough, I might catch a fragment of Olive's voice. But the current is sloshing water up my nose. I open my mouth, gagging at the spray, and will my legs to keep treading water. These earthly legs that I barely trusted a month ago.

"Leonard!" Olive says again, sounding terribly far away.

I pivot my ears toward the sound, swimming purely on instinct. Swimming toward her with all that I have.

Relief floods me when I feel the light touch of her hand, fingers waggling through the water. She grasps onto my foreleg and, with one arm, tucks me close. "I can't . . ." she says, head bobbing at the surface, "believe you . . . did that . . ."

The two of us struggle against the current, panting as we reach the shore. It's only my second experience with panting, the pink of my tongue lolling like a dog's. It alarms Stanley; gently, he mouths my neck, dragging me safely onto the mud. Olive holds him, too, until we're all out of breath, backs to the earth, staring up at swirling stars. My heart has never beat faster.

"I called your name . . ." Olive gasps, "to tell you to *stay* on shore . . . You could've been—"

"*Olive!*" Norma shouts behind us.

At the sound of her name, said with such worry, Olive begins to cry.

"You're okay," Norma says, catching up. Her knees sink to the mud, and she's cradling Olive's head, stroking her hair. "You're okay, you're okay."

I believe this is a thing that humans do: Trying to speak words into existence. Trying to change what is very clearly in front of them. Olive's jaw is clenching, and her eyes are tearing, and her ankle is swelling.

"I'm so sorry," she whispers to Norma. "I wasn't . . . I wasn't thinking, and I didn't mean to shock you, or hurt you, or—"

"Hurt me?" Norma asks, uneasy. "Are *you* hurt anywhere? Do we need to go to the hospital?"

"No hospital," Olive insists, shaking her wet head. Tears slip down her cheeks as Stanley nudges his way in, trying to lick them away. "We need to keep going. We're *so* close. I have to do this . . . this one thing right."

Norma's face is inconsolable, her voice tender. "One thing? What do you mean one thing? What's this all about?"

Olive winces, attempts to sit up. "I just thought," she says, "if I can get him there, that'll mean something, and maybe I'll feel better about everything else." Her words are flowing faster now, her sobs thicker. "And yesterday, you told me that story about my dad . . . And I thought . . . Do you know what my best day on Earth is? *Every* day that I've been with you. Every day at Turtle Beach, at the aquarium, talking to people about animals, having them listen and not make fun of me or tell me I'm 'socially unprepared for the real world.'"

Norma jerked her head back. "Who said that?"

"*Frank.*" She chokes out his name. "He told me I was weird, and that I didn't know how to make friends the right way. And I wanted to love him. I wanted it to be *good*. But who says that, Norma? How could he tell me that?"

A beat passes before Norma says, "Listen. You might not see it now, but you and me, our hearts are the same. What you did this summer? Rescuing that cat in a rowboat? Helping with the penguins and the sharks? You've got it in your blood. You're fearless.

What Frank told you? That says a heck of a lot about him, and *nothing* about you. You hear me? Hold on to yourself. Because you're good, Olive. You're good."

"Anyone there?" Q yells in the distance. "Hello?"

Norma's head spins toward his voice. "We better go. Can you stand?"

"My ankle," Olive says, grimacing.

"Oh, Lord," Norma says, seeing the swelling. "We're taking you to a hospital."

Panic spreads across Olive's face. "No, no, we have to keep moving, get to Old Faithful . . . We have to save Leonard! He's . . . No! Norma, stop!"

But Norma scoops up Olive anyway, murmuring something like, "I think you might've hit your head."

We leave my raincoat there, in the woods outside Yellowstone. I pick my way through the muck, a silhouette in front of me: a grandmother carrying her granddaughter through the night forest, the two melding into one.

Most humans believe that cats only purr when we're happy. That is largely the case. Give me a warm patch of sun and a soft blanket to knead, and listen to me hum away. But as the ambulance arrives, as amber lights flicker across the sky, I also purr to calm myself—to make the world feel safer than it is.

My instinct is to jump into the ambulance with Olive, to take a watchful seat by her stretcher. I'm midleap when the driver declares, "This is a cat-free zone." Olive, delirious with pain, reaches one hand in my direction—as she did in the river. She's whispering urgently to me, but I can't tell what she's saying. Can't tell what I'm supposed to be *doing*, as Norma climbs into the back and clasps Olive's reaching hand.

"We'll have you fixed up in no time," Norma tells her, voice shaky. But I wonder if these are just more words. A large lump grows in my throat. I wasn't aware that throats could have lumps, difficult to swallow down.

Seven hours and forty-five minutes. That's all I have—and I wanted to spend every second of it with Olive.

"She's a strong kid," Q says, after the ambulance has left. Stanley and I are flanking his sides, the three of us wallowing along the empty highway. Q dips his chin to catch my eyes, which are glowing green in the dark. "She'll be back soon. I think she will. If not, I heard Olive say something about Old Faithful? Is that where you need to go? Don't worry, my man. We'll get you home."

Exhausted, Stanley and I gather around the motor home as Q fixes the flat tire, then drives us to a campsite seven miles from Upper Geyser Basin, which—remarkably—has an open space. The whole site smells of ash and brush fire, and leaves a bitter taste on my tongue. All I can think about is Olive, strapped to the stretcher—even as Stanley does his best to distract me.

Three hours later, Q talks to Norma on speakerphone: *Fractured,* she says. Olive's ankle is fractured. And isn't this my fault? Isn't worrying Norma my fault, too? We wouldn't be here, if not for me. Olive wouldn't have been chasing my raincoat, if not for me. This whole month, worrying about my own safety— and I should've been worried about Olive's.

I'm safer on my home planet.

Maybe Olive is safer without me, too.

Under the faint light of the RV, I decide some-thing—something I should've settled on days ago. In preparation, I eat a hardy meal from the kitchen tray, licking even the crumbs. I take several long swigs of water from my dish, lapping with quick flicks of my tongue. "Gonna hop in the shower," Q says. "Then we'll leave to pick up Olive at the hospital." As soon as he closes the bathroom door, I tell Stanley goodbye. His fur is glistening in the five a.m. moonlight.

I will miss you, I say.

Me?

Yes. Yes, you. I thank him for the midafternoon naps, for the way he always breathed on me, even though it smelled.

You are leaving? he asks. *Now?*

And I say, *After one more thing.*

He helps me with the laptop. Between the two of us, between his teeth and my claws, we pry the screen open.

Words spill out of me.

Dear Olive,

You are right. I did not want to be a cat. But I am happy I was your cat, even if for a little while. These past few days, everyone has been sharing their best days on Earth, so I would like to share mine. I hope that is okay.

It is the first day. The day you saved me. I might have been scared and wet and stuck in a tree, but everything changed when I saw the boat. There is always good mixed up with the bad, and the good is you.

I have learned a great deal about water on Earth. Water pushes its way through rocks. Water carves its own path. And you are like water, Olive. Some people may call you weird. Perhaps this word is a good thing. Perhaps it is a signal, a beacon thrown up to the sky, that you are looking for others as interesting as you.

Remember that you are a remarkable human. A kind human. I used to think that being mortal meant being afraid. Although

I was never alone, I used to think that there was no one like me. But the universe is vast. And in it, I found you.

Thank you. Thank you for introducing me to your family, your life on Earth. I have promised you a goodbye, so please accept this as my farewell. I am going to protect you now, as you have always done for me. This is the only way. I must make the rest of this difficult journey alone. Please think of me sometimes, when you hold a crayon, when you eat a cheese sandwich, when you are staring at a night covered in stars.

With gratitude,

Leonard

34

Three hours before the hive arrives, I leave through the RV's back window, wedging it open with my body. The hinges creak, and for a second, the tip of my tail hooks as I hesitate on the edge. *Stay or jump. Stay or jump.*

Jump.

My front paws hit the ground with an invigorating jolt. Sunlight is already mottling the ground, yellow patches here and there, and at first I follow the pebbly path that hugs the loop road. I've checked the map, my claws tracing the zigzagged route: I'm seven miles from Old Faithful. For my body, as a cat, it will feel like a hundred. But it's better this way. Really, it is. Olive is safer without me.

Whenever fear climbs into my belly, I swallow it down. If I travel as fast as I possibly can, I'll reach the geyser just in time—and it will take all the strength I have.

The morning is moist, the forest quiet except for the suck of my paws against the sodden ground. Every step, I think of Olive. Is she awake yet? Is Q knocking on her hospital room door? Above me, songbirds begin to dart between juniper trees. I take a sharp right, curving deeper into the forest, reminding myself that I'm not a wild cat, not a puma or a lion. But there is something about the park, about mossy smells and the thickness of pines. I understand what brought me here, what attracted me to the idea of Yellowstone.

Before me are slow-moving streams, and I wade, tender-footed, through the shallowest parts. Cold water nips at my forelegs. I shake off the droplets as I leap over fallen trees, weave through tall grasses and brush. Two miles in, heart pounding, I crest a hill to see a field of wildflowers. A whole meadow of them, like the pictures said: yarrow and spring beauty, cow parsnip and woodland star. Gathering speed is difficult when you want to stop and sniff each petal, each leaf. I'm fulfilling something—a dream of mine—but all I can think is: *I hope that Olive will see this. That she'll step foot in this field and know I was here, too.*

This land is untouched. This is how Earth was before the humans. I can't stop marveling at the immensity of it all: infinite forest, infinite sky. But time is clearly of the essence—so I try to control my breath, limit my distractions, and will myself on, on, *on*. After three miles, though, it's nearly impossible to keep up the momentum. My paws stumble over rocks, skid in the mud. On my route is a small lake, with two humans fly-fishing, their green waders shining in the early morning light. One glances in my direction as she casts her line: a metallic arc against the pure blue sky.

"Did you see that?" she says to her partner.

"See what?"

"Oh. Guess I haven't had enough coffee." She shakes her head. "Thought I saw a . . . baby bear or something."

This gives me so much confidence, I can't even tell you. To be mistaken for a creature of the park! I depart from the bushes, wheatgrass thwacking my face, pushing my whiskers back. I sprint and sprint as hard as I can.

By mile six, my every muscle is aching. Even the vistas do little to soothe me. The trees and the meadows and the—

Bison!

Bursting through a pocket of shrubbery, I run almost directly into a bison. Brown, even-toed, with fur climbing all over its body. It's enormous: enormous horns, enormous tufts of fur on its head. Half of me wants to curl immediately into a ball. I can tell that my pupils are dilating, my fur standing at attention. On either side of the path are bushes too thick to cross.

So I must speak—with courage.

Puffing each tuft of fur on my bib, I say, *Excuse me*, imitating its language to the best of my ability. Should I add in a few extra grunts? Why not. I scrounge for the noise, crouching with my elbows bent. In response, the bison snorts and huffs, pounding the earth with his hooves. Which is, of course, entirely rude.

I've been awake for over twenty-seven hours. I've been running for over two and a half. And I'm only a mile from the geyser—too close to stop now.

My tail frizzes as I charge, stamping out every fear left inside me. The bison flares its nostrils, bobs its bushy head. But it moves. It *moves*.

I skirt quickly around it, unwilling to press my luck. Once I'm safely down the path, though, I say over my shoulder, *Never underestimate a cat again.*

To my intense surprise, the hive's voice answers in return.

We found you. We have been looking.

It's startling, a shock to the brain. To be out of contact with my species for so long. To miss the presence of them so much—then hear them unexpectedly, after all this time.

You are scared.

Noise shudders through my ears. *No, not scared. You just surprised me. I didn't think I could hear you from a mile away.*

We are shouting. You sound different.

I'm not sure what you—

There is emotion in your voice. And you are a cat.

Well, yes.

This does not compute. There has never been a mistake before.

I got distracted on the way here. I ended up in South Carolina.

South Carolina?

There are beaches. Quite nice, if you don't mind the sand. Or the water.

Listen to yourself.

I am. You are waiting at the geyser?

At your point of pickup, yes. You know the plan.

I know the plan. You will extend yourself over the geyser. I will jump into the geyser. I will be safe.

You must do it exactly right, despite your new circumstances.

Yes.

Hurry.

I am hurrying.

You have twelve minutes left.

I run.

Half a mile from Upper Geyser Basin, I nearly slam into a group of hikers, who part for me on the trail. "Wait," one of them says, "that's a house cat. Should he be out here?"

I appreciate her worry, I sincerely do, but when I cross the footbridge over Firehole River, Old Faithful is looming in the distance: a steaming mound of white earth, ready to blow. The hive's collective energy grows stronger with every stride I take. I'll be back with them soon. Soon Leonard will no longer be my name.

I've liked that name.

Even this body. It has a certain charm, doesn't it?

No, comes the voice of the hive.

That was rhetorical.

You did not specify.

The ground rumbles beneath my paws. Old Faithful only erupts once an hour, and I must not miss it; the hive's collective power only lasts for so long on Earth. If I botch the timing, they'll move on to pick up other travelers. Sweeping my gaze around the rocky expanse, I spot the rangers right away—dotted about the area, mixed in with the crowd of tourists. Straw hats, green trousers, gray button-up shirts. Just like the photos. Just like I was supposed to be.

I thought I'd envy them. I thought my stomach would lurch at the sight of their glittering badges. Shouldn't I be jealous of all that they are? Of everything I didn't become? *Look*, I tell myself. Look at them with their pockets! Look at them with their Swiss Army knives, their human hands, their variety of pens for writing.

I do look.

And I realize that even though I've lived in a different body, I have really and truly *lived*.

Now, the hive says. You must run now.

A grayish vapor begins streaming from the geyser in puffs; the earth shivers, little tremors up my forelegs. All my strength curls within me, and I push it out, out into the world. Sprinting. Darting across the land. Swishing through the crowd. And the rangers— they're running *after* me. Why? Why are they doing that? Honestly, I wasn't expecting a chase. What's one rogue cat in the middle of all this commotion? In the middle of tourists and summer, with the geyser about to blow?

I misjudged the attention I would draw, rushing toward a steaming pool of water, my back legs skittering under me. I'm very impressed with the rangers' physical fitness! Look how quickly they're flying!

"Clear back!" one of them yells.

"Everyone move!" another shouts. "He might be rabid!"

Rabid? They think I have *rabies*? Of all the assumptions to make, why would they jump to that one? Just because I'm foaming at the mouth, spittle flecking my chin, mad-dashing toward this geyser . . .

Tourists scatter.

A few of them scream.

Then I hear it. Her voice, piercing the crowd: *"Leonard!"*

I skid to a stop. I whip around.

Olive.

Olive on crutches—with Norma, Q, and Stanley by

her side. All of them are slipping through the fleeing crowd.

Time is running out.

"Your . . . letter!" Olive is still yelling, heavily out of breath. "I need to talk to you about your letter!"

Wait, I tell the hive, the rangers right on my tail. *I want to hear what she has to say.*

No. Go now. Run.

Olive hobbles forward, out of the crowd—ten feet away from me. "You said 'thank you for introducing me to your family.' But it's not just my family. It's yours, too."

My chest constricts.

"And I need you to know that! I really need you to know that. How much you mean to me. To all of us."

Three rangers crash into our little circle. One of them—the man with gloves—grabs me squarely by the scruff of the neck, lifting me high into the air.

Bite him, the hive says. Bite him and run.

"We're a family!" Olive gasps. "Leonard, you are my *family*!"

I blink at her, thinking.

When I was writing my ideas for human lessons, I left one important thing off the list, one thing I didn't dare hope for. *Become part of a family.* I wanted to be in a Christmas photo, for someone to dress me up with a ribbon, posing me by a tree. I wanted a stocking of my own, hung next to Olive's—and I wanted to see her, every day. Every year. Because my bucket list no longer includes things I want to do as a human. Just things I wish to do with Olive by my side.

I realize that as she limps another step toward me on her crutches. This girl. This human girl—who saved me from a flood, who just rushed a geyser, who loves me. *Love*. I can feel this, too. Half of the poetry on Earth focuses on love, and yet I didn't truly understand it until now. There is a reason that cats only purr to their humans—no one else, not even other cats.

Olive is my family. Norma, Q, and Stanley are my family. Everyone one of them feels like home.

Bite the ranger! Bite him now!

Norma is wiping tears from her cheeks—because I think she might know. About me. About everything. Q looks ashen while Stanley yelps.

"Young lady?" the ranger says, his grip still firmly on my neck. "Is this your cat?"

YOU HAVE TEN SECONDS! NINE. EIGHT.

Family.

SEVEN.

She is my family.

SIX.

"I'm his human," Olive says. "And he does *not* have rabies!"

FIVE.

I'm staying.

YOU WILL—FOUR—BECOME MORTAL—THREE.

Yes.

YOU DON'T KNOW WHAT YOU'RE—TWO.

I do.

ONE.

I'm home.

35

Maybe one day I'll be human. Maybe I'll return, after I've shed this body—after I've lived my life fully as a cat. I can still picture myself with human hands, reaching out for books, cutting the crust from peanut butter and jelly sandwiches. (I might like those even more than cheese.) But in this life, I've embraced myself for who I am.

"One heck of a cat," said a Yellowstone ranger, as Norma was writing him a check. We paid an enormous fine after the geyser incident: every cent in Olive's piggy bank and more.

"I guess it's worth it," Olive said, "to see the inside of a rangers' station."

I told her it was worth it to *stay*, here on Earth with her. With everyone.

You don't have to be born into a family to call it your own.

Now, it's two days later, and cacti are flicking by. We're somewhere in the middle of Nevada. Stanley's head is firmly out the window, his fur flapping with wind. Norma's behind the wheel, humming along with the radio. In the hospital, she started to figure it out herself—that Q and Olive weren't making a fuss over just any cat. Olive broke the news gently over the course of an hour. Norma had to sit down for a long moment. Then she got right back up again.

Apparently, if you have to recalibrate your whole way of thinking, who better to do it for than a granddaughter?

"Did you see this?" Olive says, smiling as she plunks down a newspaper. I examine the headline with powerful concentration.

HOUSE CAT (FIRST ASSUMED RABID) CHASED BY YELLOWSTONE RANGERS AFTER ATTEMPTING TO JUMP INTO OLD FAITHFUL

"Man, Leonard," Q says, plopping on the couch beside me. His coffee mug reads *America's First National Park*, and he takes a sip from it slowly, swishing the liquid around his mouth. "When you vacation, you vacation *hard*. I'm thinking that next time we do Disney World. Get you some Mickey Mouse ears. Maybe a snow globe."

Both of us squint at the image beneath the headline, and there I am, caught midstride in a tourist's photo. My eyes have never looked bigger; my ears are back as far as they can go. The cat in that picture, he's *wild*, possessed. I wish they'd gotten my better side.

"At least they got your good side," Q says.

Olive delicately folds the paper on her lap. "When we get to California, I'll have this framed. *Or* we can put it in a scrapbook—that way we can fill the rest of it up with all of our adventures. Because there will be more, I'm sure of it."

"Just as long as they don't involve geysers," Norma pipes in. "I think we've had enough water rescues for one summer. Not that you're not worth it, Leonard. You are."

"You are," Olive repeats.

"You really are," Q says.

I know the truth now: Sometimes you need to lose yourself to find yourself, even if where you find yourself is on another planet, in a strange body, with a seemingly unlimited supply of fur. I wasn't just dropped into these people's lives. I was placed here, just as they were placed into mine.

"Bowling!" Norma suddenly says, pulling into a parking lot.

My head whips toward the sound of her voice.

"What?" Olive says, genuinely confused.

"Didn't you say that Leonard wanted to bowl? Well, I plugged it into the GPS, and ta-da. I'm not sure this place allows cats, but I think we can make it work."

"This isn't just *any* cat," Q says, perfecting the line. "This is Leonard, Champion of Geysers, Wearer of Raincoats, Best Cat of the Aquarium. You ready, kid?"

And we are.

I'm surprised to learn that bowling lanes are delightfully slick. I like the noises, the smell of popcorn in the background. I like that when I glance up, after watching my ball teeter down the lane, my humans are there. My *family* is there.

Olive isn't even embarrassed to bring in her cat on a leash.

"Maybe it is weird," she tells me, scratching right

behind my ears. "Maybe *I'm* weird, but that's okay. You taught me that."

Then she touches her dry nose to mine.

I have been thinking lately about the idea of soul mates—identifying your soul in another. How we may not be made of the same materials, of fur and air, but we can recognize each other across a crowded room. When we catch each other's glance, our souls will say, *Yes, I know you,* and *Yes, this feels like home.* I understand what it feels like now, to know a place. To give yourself up to gravity.

To rescue someone—just as much as they rescue you.

After everything—after the road trip and Yellowstone and summer—there is snow. It spills over the backyard in magnificent clumps, falling gently from the sky. This is Maine. This is our house, a few miles from the ocean; we can see the water from Olive's bedroom—*our* bedroom, which we've painted yellow like our raincoats.

"Leonard!" Olive calls from the foyer. "You coming?"

Downstairs in the kitchen, eggs are frying. Lifting my nose to the air, I can smell them: the pancakes, too. Olive says that her mom always makes pancakes on Christmas. "Sometimes she puts strawberries in them." Whatever they taste like, I'm thrilled just to be here, on a human holiday, with my human family. Because this *is* my family—each one of them. Olive's mother, with her denim dresses and kind smile.

Norma, who learned how to scratch underneath my chin, in exactly the way I like. And Olive, who finally told her mother about Frank. About what he said.

Now Frank is back in California. Frank is *staying* in California, alone, without Olive's mother.

And we are staying here.

I stretch on the windowsill, a full arch in my back, then pitter-patter downstairs—where Olive is waiting, black boots laced to her knees. She's dressed in layers: fleece under her overalls, hat over her daisy barrettes. My fur coat has grown thick, thicker than I imagined it could, which comes in handy for the outdoors. Olive's mom has installed a small cat door that latches at night, so during the day I may come and go as I please; there are chipmunks to chase and trees to climb. (I have figured out, now, how to make my way down.)

"Follow me for a second," Olive says, using the human door. I trail her onto the porch, icy air nipping at my paws. We shouldn't stay out for too long, not in this weather, but we love watching the snow fall together. Another human thing. Another way I'm experiencing the world. Before us are snow-covered trees. Maine is like Yellowstone in so many ways: the green of the land, the way forests unfold like a human opening their hands. And I wonder, in all the time I was trying to get to Yellowstone, if I was actually trying to get here instead.

Olive's breath clouds in the cold. "I can't believe it's already Christmas."

Neither can I. Olive returned to school in September, which was difficult in some ways, but she's made so many friends this year—human friends. Friends who can properly digest cheese sandwiches, who can go to the movies without being stuffed in a jacket. It's brought us even closer; she can return home, fix a snack for the two of us, and tell me all about her day.

We have so many days left, so much time to flip through the pages of books and watch *I Love Lucy* and camp together under incredibly blue skies. I'm sure when it's all over, I'll wish for more time. Just another month, or a day, or an hour. I will grasp on to life because I know nothing else. But then another thought will come: that I have lived. That I've been given the privilege of existing in this form, on this Earth, with these people—this family who has loved me for everything that I am.

I am Leonard. *Her* Leonard. Just as she is my Olive.

"Norma knitted you a scarf," she says, tucking her hands into her enormous pockets. "I mean, *Gran* knitted you a scarf. She said I can call her Gran, if I want. Anyway, it took her a really, really long time—which is why I'm telling you now. Give her extra headbutts, okay? Now close your eyes. I mean it, Leonard, close them!"

So I do, and when I open them again, when I look up, there is a perfectly circular umbrella suspended above our heads.

"Do you like it?" Olive says. "I thought you should have your very own." She leans down to me, petting my coat—and I couldn't have asked for any more than this. Olive is still rescuing me, bit by bit, even now.

You should hear this, if you're still listening. I don't understand everything about being human, but I do know a great deal about the soul: how it travels and travels, until it finds someone who feels like home. I'm home now. I'm never letting go.

Olive places the umbrella handle into my paw, helping me grasp it. "Hold on tight," she says—and to all of it, to every moment, I do.

ACKNOWLEDGMENTS

People say that writing a book "takes a village," but since this novel has an alien theme, I guess I'll rephrase: it takes a galaxy.

First, thank you to my family, who've encouraged and supported me—and didn't bat a single eyelid when I said, very calmly and professionally, that I was pitching a book about an alien cat. To my husband, Jago, for tea and copious TV breaks; you are the penguin to my penguin guard. To Dad, for steadily talking me down on a weekly basis and for just being there. I appreciate you. And to Mom, for everything else; this book would not exist without your wisdom, energy, and obscure scientific knowledge.

Huge thanks to my agent, Claire Wilson. Your unwavering support of this book was a life raft in a hurricane. Everyone at RCW, including Miriam Tobin, has been incredible. And, of course, I've had the privilege of working with the brilliant Tom Bonnick, whose careful attention has made this book immeasurably kinder, braver, and just, well, better. Thank you to the inimitable Susan Van Metre for her guidance and belief in Leonard. You are all such bright stars.

Everyone at Nosy Crow and Walker Books—you launched my middle-grade career with the greatest care. I couldn't ask for more wonderful publishers. To the booksellers, teachers, reviewers, and readers who helped *I, Cosmo*, my middle-grade debut, into the world: you're magical. Thank you to Waterstones for giving me a one-in-a-million chance.

There are a number of people who've been there since the very beginning, and a number who came after. I honestly adore each and every one of you. Grandma Pat, the staff at McIntyre's, Ellen Locke, Sandy Johnson, Miss Kim, Erin Cotter: three cheers for everyone! Big thanks to Q for the Myrtle Beach memories and for the name.

Now, are you ready? Here are all the cats. Bella, Duncan, Mini Me, Bailey, Sooty, Moonlight, Bert, Mister Smitty, Whiskers, Miss Kitty, Charlie, Abby Cat, that orange cat I used to pet in Camden, Cyrano, and Snowball: I love you, I love you, I love you.

You may be asking: Where can I find a cat like Leonard? You're in luck! Almost every shelter has excellent kitties waiting for good homes. (These cats *might* not be aliens—but they're still filled with love.)

And finally, Leonard really is a family name. Pop, I miss you. Charlie would be so proud.

Enjoyed Leonard's story?
Keep an eye out for Carlie Sorosiak's next book,
about a genius mouse on a mission to save
her friends. Told in letters,

ALWAYS, CLEMENTINE

invites readers to ponder what it means
to be good, and to see that goodness
isn't proportional to size.

ABOUT THE AUTHOR

CARLIE SOROSIAK is the author of *I, Cosmo* and two novels for young adults. She teaches at Savannah College of Art and Design and lives in Atlanta.